SCARY STORIES FOR KIDS

SPINE-TINGLING TALES FOR BRAVE KIDS WHO LIKE SPOOKY STORIES

NATHAN SNYDER

ISBN: 979-8-88768-009-5

CONTENTS

INTRODUCTION

Hey, all you kids! Ready to get totally scared? Good, because here come 13 super scary stories to frighten your socks off! They're not all about Halloween, but quite a few of them are because that's simply the darkest, most evil, scariest time of the year.

Even if you do manage to get a lot of delicious candy when you go trick or treating, you'd still better be very careful at Halloween - you'll find out why soon enough.

Pumpkins that attack kids, bobbing for apples when your head suddenly gets stuck underwater, and all the crazy creatures that surround "Creepy Campground" where your parents decide to camp - you get the idea.

By the way: all these stories are true (except for the fact that we took out some of the most horrific details that would surely keep you up all night). And do you know why there are 13 super scary stories here? Because most people agree that 13 is the unluckiest number that ever existed!

CHAPTER 1.

TRICK OR TREAT AT MRS. KORNER'S VERY DARK HOUSE

I was lucky to grow up in the suburbs on a quiet street with a bunch of beautiful huge trees. In one direction, there was a big avenue not far away, with a wave of cars that passed every three minutes when the traffic signal changed at the top of the hill. In the other direction, there were a few houses, and then the infrequently used railroad tracks.

On the other side of the tracks, there was a solitary spooky house that belonged to Mrs. Korner. She lived alone with lots of dogs that rarely stopped barking and howling. After you passed her dark house, the road stretched on forever into the countryside.

My older sister, my younger brother, and I all loved the place where we grew up, especially because there were lots of other kids to play with after school, and a ton of squirrels for our dog Mike to chase every day of his life. Once, my mom told us, Mike finally caught one of those fast furry animals while we were away at school, but he was so surprised at his rare success that he just opened his mouth and let the squirrel run free!

Our parents, however, and all the other kids' parents as well, warned us to never, ever cross the railroad tracks without one of them, since there was no barrier to lower when the trains came speeding by twice a day. They told us sadly that once upon a time, a young boy, almost the same age as us, had been run over by the train when his bicycle wheel somehow got stuck between the train tracks. That was the saddest, scariest story I ever heard up to that point in my life.

But you really need to know about the kids we played with every day after school in our peaceful neighborhood. There was Brooks, who was my brother's age, and his older sister, Darlene, who was the same age as my sister. Brooks was the only kid on the block who could run faster than me, and he always reminded me about that just to make sure I didn't forget.

Then there was Henry and his sister Flora. Henry was by far the smartest kid in our class, but you probably wouldn't say he was the most handsome as his glasses were a little too thick, and his enormous pants were always sliding down, which meant he spent most of the time pulling them back up.

Closer to the big avenue lived my best friend Carl and his younger sister, Karina. They had an older brother Mac, but we rarely caught a glimpse of him because he was always working to make a few extra bucks to buy a fancy car. One of the reasons Carl was my best friend was that he was not only nice, but also had all the best sports equipment you can possibly imagine, like a regulation NBA basketball hoop in his driveway, and every kind of ball (American football, basketball, softball, and an authentic whiffleball) you could only dream of having. Also, his mother made the best hot buttered popcorn you ever tasted. I stuffed my mouth with it and wiped my buttery hands on my shorts when I was invited there once a week to watch a movie.

Of course, life wasn't just a bowl full of cherries, as my dad used to say. Carl's mother took us all aside once and told us always to watch out for her son: Carl was an epileptic, and if he had an attack all of a sudden and started to swallow his tongue, then we should run as fast as we could to get her or somebody to help.

"But don't ever put your finger in his mouth when he's having an attack, or he'll bite it and you might lose it!" She alerted us dramatically. We didn't even know how to pronounce Carl's condition, but we decided to appoint Brooks as our runner if Carl had an unexpected attack.

Finally, there was Lucas who lived on the other side of Carl. I don't even remember now how many sisters Lucas had, but he had a crew. One was named Candy, and you can imagine all the kidding she got when Halloween rolled around.

Oh, I forgot to tell you about Loraine and Chip who lived on the other side of the street from us, closest to the railroad tracks and Mrs. Korner's house. I always had a crush on Loraine, but now that I think about it, she probably only spoke to me about five times in five years. And then one day, they moved away. I still don't know what Chip's real name was.

As Halloween approached, the scary stories about why Mrs. Korner lived all alone in that very dark house with her constantly barking dogs growing more numerous and ever scarier. Maybe Mrs. Korner had murdered her husband late one night, and nobody found out. Or maybe she preferred living only with dogs and not people since she could loudly order the dogs to do whatever she wanted.

Another kid from outside our neighborhood, with an even more fertile imagination, informed us of his humble opinion: Mrs. Korner was an ex-convict (which meant she had spent time in jail after committing some terrible crime long ago) who now helped other lawless fugitives escape by hiding them in the shadowy barn behind her house before they hopped a train to freedom. We found out many years later that one of these stories was mostly true.

When Halloween finally arrived at the end of October, it was getting to be extremely cold and windy, and naturally darker and darker, as it was the end of the fall season. Yet all the houses on our suburban street were lit up and decorated with colorful displays, carved pumpkins with glowing lights inside, and plenty of those fake spider webs to add to the excitement and scariness.

And if you're anything like me, you'll agree that Halloween is one of the best times of the year, mainly because after going trick or treating to only ten houses or so, you come home with about a month's worth of sweet stuff in your bag, and you didn't have to share most of that cavity-causing candy with your siblings.

I'll never forget when I was about ten years old, my older sister and some of the other senior kids in the group like Flora decided it was my turn to go first across the railroad tracks to Mrs. Korner's dark door to ring the doorbell at Halloween. And if that didn't work, I was supposed to then rap on the door knocker, which would certainly set the old woman's pack of dogs howling and snarling beyond belief.

To tell you the truth, looking at Mrs. Korner's sinister house from the outside, it was the darkest, most ill-kept house anybody in our group of kids had ever laid eyes on, including in all the scary movies we'd seen, even with every kind of frightful special effect that you see nowadays. On top of that, the house was surrounded by foreboding trees, including some called weeping willows, which I'd read were often planted on old gravestones as a symbol of mourning for the dead!

One other reason it was so dark and horrifying was that the front door had a kind of broken lamp above it that never completely worked. It was always flickering and sputtering like it was alive, yet defective. I know because I rode my bike back and forth as fast as I could past Mrs. Korner's very dark house many times just to check.

That Halloween - when I was elected to go ahead of the rest and knock on Mrs. Korner's somber door - was also the first year that we didn't have any adults to accompany us. They had decided that my sister and some of the elder girls like Flora and Darlene were old enough to look after the younger kids. They never knew that there was probably a killer hiding somewhere on Mrs. Korner's property.

When I finally worked up the nerve to approach the old woman's door, the dogs close behind it were already howling in rabid delight. My face was burning, with my breath coming in great rushes. I felt like I was the only kid in the world facing off against a supernatural monster. In fact, I was - since my sister and all the other older kids were well behind me, hiding behind all kinds of hideous masks in the dim light.

To tell you the truth, I was so petrified that I almost peed in my pants! But in the end, I held out because I wasn't sure which was worse: getting killed by Mrs. Korner and her dogs or having my sister and her friends see me wet my pants. Also, somewhere in the deep recesses of my mind, I still imagined receiving a shower of candy corn, that sweetest of all orange, yellow, and white triangular candy that melts in your mouth on Halloween.

Finally, I rang the bell and waited. The dogs just on the other side bayed more ominously, some with high laughing barks, and others with deep, rich, child-eating barks. I looked quickly back at the other kids (who'd retreated even a little more) and saw my sister gesticulating madly to bang on the door knocker.

Sweat trickled and then ran down my back under my costume, even though it was almost freezing on that fateful October 31 night. As an obedient younger brother, I abruptly banged the door knocker three times as hard as I could. Then the pack of wild dogs became strangely quiet as the door cracked open just a sliver.

"Who is it?" Shouted out a riveting baritone voice.

I could feel my own squeaky voice coming out of my gaping mouth, almost on its own accord, "It's me! It's us! We're just trick or treating."

The booming voice answered, "Go away! And don't ever come back here again!"

That didn't sound at all like Mrs. Korner, although come to think of it, none of us had ever spoken with her before, let alone seen her in person. The door slammed shut.

At that moment, Flora - who was obviously braver than all the rest of the kids - marched confidently to the dark door and rapped on the knocker four solid times. A minute passed, and the door creaked slowly open again. This time, we could see a tall shadowy form silhouetted in the door frame, a billowing dress blowing behind her. But the booming voice was clearly that of a large man or something from another realm beyond this earth.

"I thought I told you all to go away, and never come here again!" The form demanded.

Flora spoke clearly, "We're only trick or treating! After all, it is Halloween, in case you didn't know."

Before we knew it, a shower of candy flew through the door, and then it banged shut in a shower of dust.

As the dogs began to bark madly again from behind the closed door, all the kids scrambled in the dirt driveway for whatever candy we could quickly find, and then grabbed each other's sweaty hands and headed for the hills.

Actually, we ran together arm in arm across the railroad tracks, glimmering in the cold night air. If any of us fell while sprinting, we were immediately scooped up by brothers and sisters. None of us stopped running until we got home. After we made it into our houses, locked the doors, and blabbered to our parents about what had happened, not one of us could sleep until way after midnight.

As you can probably guess, our parents didn't pay much attention to our horror story. They said something like, "Well, it sounds like you had a lot of fun." And, "don't forget to brush your teeth a little bit more than usual tonight because of all that candy!" Lucky for us, the next day was Saturday. But nobody came out to play on our street like normal that day. My sister and I guessed it was probably because the weather was unusually cloudy and dreary, with the wind whipping through the trees.

A week later, we saw a police car pass our place and stop on the other side of the railroad tracks at Mrs. Korner's very dark house, even though it was broad daylight. Later, my dad - who knew all the other dads on our street - got a call, after which he told us we couldn't go outside for the rest of the weekend.

Naturally, as a kid, you try to find out about all the crazy stuff going on with your neighbors, although some somber secrets never come out. It turned out that there really *was* a runaway fugitive hiding in Mrs. Korner's barn, and the reports said he used some of the old lady's clothes to disguise himself. In the end, we learned he wasn't truly a killer but had just stolen somebody's new car.

The police also found the terrified Mrs. Korner tied up in a chair in the back of the barn, but luckily, she was all right. As far as I know, until we finally moved to another house, nobody ever went trick or treating at Mrs. Korner's house again. And I never found out what happened to that fugitive either, but I'd rather not think about it too much if you don't mind.

CHAPTER 2.

ATTACK OF THE ASSASSIN PUMPKINS

Who doesn't love pumpkins on Halloween? These gorgeous orange orbs have become symbolic of the late-October fest all kids know and love. From this humble vegetable that ripens in the fall, we can easily take out the seeds, roast and salt them, and have a nice healthy snack.

But that's certainly not all. We can also scoop out the pumpkin's innards and leave it to our parents (or the local bakery) to cook up a storm, resulting in some of the best pie on earth. In case you haven't yet tried this, it's called pumpkin pie. That slightly sour interior is easily sweetened, especially when the chef decides to conjure up some homemade whipped cream as a topping, or simply deposits a huge scoop of vanilla ice cream on the side of your piece of steaming autumn pie.

For many families, carving pumpkins is the real highlight of Halloween, in particular since the vegetable can easily provide dramatic faces when carved, some scarier than others, which are coolly highlighted by sticking a candle inside. This causes an eerie, otherworldly glow on your front porch to greet the neighborhood's trick-or-treaters.

Considering how cute and round pumpkins are when they start in the garden, can you possibly imagine that some of them end up as evil assassins? That's right - in search of revenge, they actually come directly in pursuit of kids who smash other pumpkins, perhaps thinking that's a kind of Halloween trick.

Whether or not you've ever heard of a rock band called the "Smashing Pumpkins," you probably know that breaking the pretty pumpkins that people have neatly carved to celebrate Halloween is a way for some kids to get back at those who don't offer the kind of candy they crave. This is the part of the equation called "trick" (when the proper treat doesn't arrive in your hands)!

So, there once was a group of pals who'd all just entered the fifth grade. Gus, Marley, and Isabella were their names. Isa happened to be a huge fan of *Harry Potter*, and anything else remotely magical, while Marley was basically hooked on video games - constantly competing and playing on either his cell phone, tablet, or whatever device might be handy. Last but certainly not least, Gus was a bit more aggressive than the others, always getting into fights and scrapes of one kind or another at school.

When Halloween came around that particular year, all Marley could suddenly think about was the odd pleasure he got from breaking pumpkins. In fact, the first time he'd ever broken one of those fat veggies was by accident. He was carving one together with his grandpa and when asked to carry a big bulging one they'd spent hours on, creating a horrific leering mask, he'd accidentally dropped it on the doorstep. The orange globe had exploded on the cement into a hundred pieces!

On the one hand, Marley was sad that he'd disappointed his grandpa, as he always seemed to be disappointing the adults in his life - especially his parents who'd recently split up. On the other hand, when the pumpkin fell hard to the ground below him, Marley heard a satisfying thud - not quite an eruption, but something solid and slightly destructive that gave him an unexpected feeling of power and control.

One thing that Marley did notice about his grandpa, especially since his grandma had passed away the previous winter, was how much time the old man spent tending to his precious vegetable garden, in particular his prize pumpkin patch. Marley's grandpa raised all kinds of pumpkins, and he enjoyed roasting pumpkin seeds, dabbled at making pumpkin pie (though it would obviously never be the same as his grandma's award-winning dessert), and reserved the best, biggest, and most orange orbs for Marley and his pals to carve at Halloween.

When Gus and Isa arrived at his place that Halloween in the early evening, the former was wearing one of his favorite "Brawl Star" character costumes - that of El Primo - while the latter showed up as a magical anime girl. Marley was dressed up as a sinister assassin, totally ready to go out into the neighborhood in search of his favorite candies, and some juicy, freshly-carved pumpkins to destroy. Of course, he didn't reveal his wish to Isa or Gus, knowing that these two kids were a bit more strait-laced than him.

The first house the trio visited that night for their trick-or-treating pleasure had a brilliant row of freshly-carved pumpkins lining a porch that led to the front door. Marley's eyes widened in delight. The costumed friends rang the doorbell, received a handful of candy each from the kind residents, and were prepared to move on to the next house. But Marley lingered, eying one fat pumpkin in particular.

"Let's go," Isa suggested.

"Wait just a minute for me - I'm just going to quickly smash one of these pumpkins!" Marley's excited voice shot back.

"Don't do that, Marley - please, we'll get into trouble," implored Gus.

But before they knew it, a plump pumpkin lay completely smashed on the porch, Marley's hands were coated in pumpkin juice, and he had a devilish grin flickering on his face.

Gus had pulled Marley out of quite a few fights at school. Why Marley always had to get nervous and then start swinging at others who only slightly bullied him - after all, he was a bit chubby - Gus didn't really know. But they considered themselves best friends who liked a lot of the same things, like burgers and salty fries, soccer, and a game called "Subway Surfer."

The trio of costumed kids moved along swiftly to the next house, which appeared much bigger than the others on the block, with a darker doorway and many more illuminated pumpkins than they'd ever seen. Gus looked sideways at Marley and was surprised to see him rubbing his hands and grinning. Isa rang the doorbell, and an older man answered. It was difficult to see his face at first as he wore a hooded jacket.

His voice was smooth and welcoming: "Please, kids - come all the way into my house. I have plenty of special treats waiting for you inside."

As any kid would do, they greedily grabbed enormous handfuls of chocolate bars, lollipops, and hard candies until their Halloween bags bulged to the breaking point. At the same time, they saw that the living room was lined with oversized pumpkins, their shadows flickering and dancing on the dark walls.

At that moment, the older man with the hidden face excused himself to answer the telephone ringing in the next room.

He was only gone for a moment, but Marley blurted out to his two pals, "Let's break some of these pumpkins together!"

Isa shot back, "Marley, are you crazy? That man will be right back, and this time we'll really be in hot water!"

"Isa, forget about being in hot water - I'm really fast - just watch this!" Marley exclaimed as he lifted a glowing pumpkin over his head.

Before anybody could talk sense to Marley, or do anything at all to stop him, he'd already brought the pumpkin he held crashing down, shattering it on the smooth wood floor they stood on.

This time, Marley looked a little less confident in himself, maybe knowing that he'd done something completely out of line. At that precise moment, they didn't see the man, but they certainly heard his booming voice.

"Do you kids like spicy cooking? I hope so! And, do you kids like crazy computer games? Great, because you're going to get a taste of each right now. Good luck, by the way, and try to remember next time that pumpkins - and the people that carefully carve them - are supposed to be your friends," the hooded man's voice echoed in the room.

Surely, when Marley destroyed pumpkins, he never really thought about the people who spent time planning their designs, cutting open the pumpkin top and taking out all the gooey insides, and then cautiously carving a face that captured joy or terror in some creative way. When Marley detonated pumpkins on the ground, he only thought about how it made him feel momentarily better, as he remembered the other kids who bullied him, and his parents fighting one another with cutting words.

Now, he was told to think about the pumpkins and the people who spent time carving them. But he didn't have much time to think about anything at that moment because suddenly the room started to whirl around, and he and Gus and Isa all fell in a heap. As the room rotated, leaving them all desperately dizzy, the chamber also started to get unbearably hot, almost like they were cooking. Then, just like that, stinging particles of something hard were flying in their faces and pinging their skin. Gus got a little taste of the stinging particles - they were salty.

Though they couldn't see him, the man's booming voice came blasting back at them: "This is what it feels like to be cooked in a pan like pumpkin seeds for people to eat!"

Abruptly, the room stopped spinning, and the trio could immediately feel and see a series of shiny metal cooking tools beating them on the backs and stomachs as they helplessly rolled by on the floor. Just as Marley was trying to take a gasp of much-needed air, he was impolitely punched in the stomach by one of the metal tools. His breath rushed out of him, and he felt dangerously close to passing out.

The thunderous voice sounded again: "Now you know what it's like for pumpkins to be made into a pie!"

At last, Isa struggled to her feet, only to have the rug rudely pulled out from under her. Gus tried to prevent her from falling again in the middle of the chaos, but he was too late.

Due to all his experience playing computer games, Gus always thought very fast. But this real-life horror story inside the man's ample house was all too rapid, even for the best of computer game players. Gus could only watch in terror as an invisible hand seemed to lift Marley's limp body off the floor and throw him roughly back down.

"Now you know how it feels for an innocent pumpkin to be thrown and broken into a hundred pieces by a person who's not thinking straight about Halloween!" The man's trembling voice shook through the heated room, pumpkin pulp and juice dripping from the slippery walls, as colored lights flashed.

The last thing she knew, Isa and her two friends were being roughly dumped on a moving belt and scrubbed and brushed with oversized implements, almost like they were exiting a car wash. When they came to a halt, they found themselves lying together on the front step of the large house at the end of the street, with a row of freshly-carved pumpkins leering at them. They were all wet but seemed to be sound - without any broken bones.

"Oh, my goodness, what just happened in there?" Exclaimed Isa to her two pals.

"On the one hand, that was almost the attack of the assassin pumpkins - and way better than any computer game I've ever played in my whole life! On top of that, it looks like most of our candy is still here, though it's a bit soggy," reasoned Gus. "On the other, it was also *really scary*, all around."

Marley concluded, "It's all my fault. I couldn't control myself, and when I broke that guy's special pumpkin in his own house, I got us all into big trouble - and you two didn't do anything wrong."

At that moment, they heard the man's deep voice again from just inside the dark doorway. They looked up at his towering figure as his hood slowly slid down around his broad neck. They stared at a powerful shape that soared above them. Without the hood, they could see his head was a perfectly round, bright orange pumpkin, with a wide one-toothed smile.

The mysterious figure spoke slowly, "It's never only one person's fault. And one thing you should know by now, after playing so many computer games in your young lives, is that you always get a second chance. I'm not so sure you'll get a third, but some people do get lucky. By all means, please come trick or treating again here next year!"

CHAPTER 3.

LET'S BOB FOR APPLES

You may quickly recognize the nickname Bob from your uncle, your gym teacher, or just the guy next door. But did you know that bobbing for apples is one of the most cherished and original Halloween party activities? It seems kind of silly to stick your head in a large container of freezing water during the late fall season to try and snag a floating apple between your teeth so that you can win a minor prize. But that's what bobbing for apples means. And your parents will tell you that's the real fun of Halloween!

And just in case you're reading this late at night, imagine that it's also possible to get your head stuck underwater in that very same container! Who'd have thought a relatively small bucket of water is enough to be the end of you? Halloween should be lots of fun, without that kind of crazy risk.

Perhaps it's worth looking at the origin of this fine Halloween tradition to understand how far we've come from the real origins of the activity. Did you know that bobbing for apples has been a fall custom for centuries? But even though we see bobbing for apples at Halloween parties and festivals everywhere nowadays, its roots are more related to love and romance than anything to do with modern trick or treating.

It appears that this type of bobbing began as a courting ritual in old England. That doesn't mean that anybody was playing badminton, basketball, or tennis on a court. Instead, young guys were doing their best to win over young ladies, with music, poetry, wit, and lots of charm. It usually happened in a yard, also called a court, where one of the girl's relatives (normally a sharp-eyed aunt or uncle) could keep a close eye on them, looking down on the courtyard from above.

It seems that there were a few versions of this game. One group of rules said that each specific apple was assigned to a possible partner. The person bobbing would try to bite into the special apple associated with the partner he or she preferred. If the bobber could secure the apple in their teeth on the very first try, the couple was sure to get hooked. If the bobber succeeded on the second try, the relationship could proceed, but love would probably fade. If success came on the third try, the relationship simply wouldn't work. In other words, it was doomed to fail!

Doom - now there's a good word for Halloween. Doom means a terrible fate or destiny is coming that you can't avoid. Just wait until our next story really unfolds! But let's take our time. You should know that in another version of the bobbing game, the first person to successfully snag any apple with their teeth would be the winner and thus the first to marry.

A related superstition was that the winner could place the apple under their pillow that night, and their future soul mate would come to visit them in their dreams that very same night. I know that if I put an apple under my pillow at night, the uncomfortable lump would mean my dreams wouldn't be very good. What do you think?

Anyway, on Halloween, Ava and her best friend Mia, both 12 years old, were invited to a friend's Halloween party. Mia knew very well that Ava had eyes for a certain guy in their class named Everett, a charming, funny, and good-looking hockey player who'd certainly be at the same party. The only problem was that Raya, another girl obviously interested in Everett, would also be there. She and Ava were rivals and enemies. They didn't like each other at all.

The night of the party rolled around, and wouldn't you know that there was a huge full moon shining down on the activities? The party hosts had decided to hold some of the messier activities outside in the backyard. Bobbing for apples would definitely be there since that activity led to water being sprayed and splashed everywhere, as the contestants tried to get their teeth on the best and brightest apples to win certain prizes.

Raya made it clear that she wanted to win at everything, especially if any competitive activity involved a girl like Ava who she viewed as yet another obstacle in her pursuit of world domination. Ava was a good sport, however, and agreed to compete in the first round of bobbing for apples in the same bucket and at the same time as Raya.

Everett and Mia looked on with interest as the two girl competitors allowed their hands to be lightly tied behind their backs so they could only use their mouths to bob for and bite into elusive apples. When the signal came for the two girls to begin bobbing, the action was fast and furious. Ava tried not to pay too much attention to Raya and focused on biting into one apple that looked like it was about the same size as her mouth - even though it was tough to tell the actual dimensions with her head underwater at night, despite the moon high overhead.

Just as Ava closed in on her prized apple, she felt the firm grip of a foreign hand on the back of her head. The hand she couldn't see gripped the back of her head tightly, forcing her further underwater, and eventually making her panic.

She finally fought loose from the evil hand and managed to get her head out of the water bucket, choking and wheezing from the effort. At that moment, through soggy eyes, she saw Raya standing triumphantly with an apple between her teeth.

Everett and Mia rushed to Ava's side.

"What happened? Are you alright?" Everett asked Ava in a comforting, concerned voice.

"Somebody was pushing me down under the water. Was that Raya's hand holding me down?" Ava gasped while coughing up some water.

"We could only see you struggling under the water by yourself!" Mia exclaimed.

At that moment, Ava decided that she'd had enough of bobbing for apples, especially since she was exhausted after fighting against the strange force. Plus, Everett paid more attention to her after the bobbing incident. But they stayed to watch the next round of the game, which featured Raya again - she simply *had* to win more prizes. This time, however, it was Raya's turn to suffer.

She ducked her head under the water just like before but seemed to get stuck there in the small bucket. While her opponent - a girl they didn't know - popped up with an apple between her teeth, Raya appeared to fight against an invisible enemy. Her body shook as if her hair or maybe her hairband was caught by something under the water's surface. She finally tore her head from the bucket, staggered a step or two back, and fell to the ground, spitting and coughing out of control.

Kids and adults alike rushed to Raya's side, asking if she was all right. Everett, Mia, and even Ava were all worried about Raya's dramatic reaction. After some minutes, Raya recovered somewhat and demanded to know whose powerful hand had held her head under the water against her will, almost making her die in that small bucket - at least she claimed.

Raya steamed with anger and started screaming at all those around her. She shouted, "I hate all of you! I can't believe someone tried to hurt me - kill me even - just so that I wouldn't win at bobbing for apples!"

One of the hosts tried to comfort her and reason with her, but Raya stormed away from the party, yelling and kicking chairs.

The scariest part of the whole affair was seeing a person who couldn't control her anger - who seemed almost like a person possessed by a violent spirit that entered her body from outside. If she kicked a chair in anger, she could easily kick a dog or a person as well.

Raya missed the next two weeks of school. Ava and Mia even overheard some of their teachers talking about Raya's meltdowns and tantrums in school. The teachers wondered out loud why she was so stressed out and had problems completing the work she was meant to do at home.

What kinds of problems was Raya perhaps having at home, and how could the teachers help her handle the stress? The two friends probably weren't supposed to hear all that stuff, but because they were good snoops, they did anyway.

When Raya finally came back to school two weeks later, she seemed a little calmer and less competitive than before. She even reached out to Ava, not exactly to apologize, but to share her dislike of bobbing for apples. Both of the girls spoke privately of the feeling of doom they'd experienced when the mysterious and powerful hand then held their heads underwater. Other outsiders couldn't really understand this kind of supernatural event, but together the two of them could.

In the end, Raya and Ava even stood together to cheer on the school's hockey team. They watched Everett rush around with the puck, and try a big left-handed slapshot, causing his opponents to flinch, but it didn't result in a goal. Raya decided that she didn't want to compete all the time for everything as it just made her tired and caused others to be upset with her.

She tried sleeping on an apple to get closer to Everett, but all that happened was she lost a fair amount of sleep because of the discomfort. At the end of the day, Everett still fell for Ava, while Raya attracted the attention of the hockey team's goalkeeper, Teddy, who was actually quite cute when he finally removed his goalie mask.

CHAPTER 4.

CLICKING CLAWS AT CREEPY CAMPGROUND

When your parents tell you that they've decided to take you on another kind of summer vacation - just this summer for a change - which is going to be tent camping in a series of national and state parks filled with wild animals: beware! Your flashlight and penknife alone won't be quite enough to defend you. And those old kung fu movies you guys watch sometimes - believe me, those combination moves you saw the stuntmen pull off won't help you a bit in the primeval forest.

It all started for me when my parents made a similar announcement. All those great summer vacations my family used to take at the beach - we went bodysurfing, built sand castles (and once even tried to dig a hole to China as our dad suggested so that he could read a chapter of his book in peace), threw the frisbee, played touch football with my uncle who insisted on smearing his entire (and I might add, slightly chubby) body with the greasiest coconut oil ever so he'd avoid getting touched, devoured at least three rapidly-melting ice cream cones a week, and on Saturday night, went to the boardwalk along the beach, where there were lots of fun games like mini-golf, and rides like those spinning tea cups you sit in and feel queasy – all of this fun was suddenly out the window.

This summer, we were told that we were going tent camping at a string of parks - no ifs, ands, or buts, according to our mom. The first thing we had to learn to do, and practice, was setting up our tents in the backyard. Since I come from a big family, that meant I would have to share a tent with my older brother Michael, while my two older sisters (Lisa and Sally) would share a tent next to us. That was the plan at least. But if you saw the way my sisters usually disagreed about everything, you knew it was going to be tough to share a cramped space.

Next, our dad told us that we had to learn how to use a compass.

We answered in unison, "Dad, you must be kidding. Everybody has GPS on their cell phones nowadays!"

He immediately replied, "Where we're going, there definitely won't be any internet. Indeed, in some of the parks, we're going to visit, we may have trouble finding running water."

Michael then sneered, "You mean we're going to visit some parks on other planets?"

But sometimes my dad was a little too serious for his own good. "Michael, we're going to be staying right here on earth. Our ultimate destination is going to be the Upper Peninsula in Michigan!" He announced excitedly.

Well, that was a bit far for those of us who lived as we did in the magnificent state of Maine, which happened to have a snappy slogan, "Life As It Should Be."

The next job we were assigned before the big trip was to read up on the wild animals that we might meet in some of these creepy campgrounds.

Again, Michael chimed in, "Hey, we're already out of school - no more reading for me this year!"

However, my sister Lisa and I took this task a little more seriously. Besides the comical but very large and territorial moose where we lived, what kinds of savage animals might we encounter on our trip out west?

We checked online, and in the end, didn't actually read too much. But we certainly saw a lot of great mug shots and pictures. There was the ever-elusive bobcat, but it didn't seem to bother too much with humans - preferring instead to munch on smaller prey like tasty voles, mice, and sometimes a chipmunk for dessert. In the state of Wisconsin, besides many kinds of cheese, they have something called a badger, which looked really nasty. But it seemed that if you didn't actually try to enter its narrow burrow together with it, you'd probably be all right.

When we got to Montana on the map, we saw wolves and coyotes that gobbled down prairie dogs, grizzly bears, and bison that now and then charged cars (and I'm not talking about money!) in Yellowstone National Park because they were so nearsighted that they thought cars were their enemies. Then, my sister, Lisa told me that we'd gone too far. Literally speaking, she said - we're not going all the way to Montana - until next summer!

One thing that Michigan's Upper Peninsula had that you should apparently watch out for was abundant black bears. We noted that they liked to come into campgrounds to look for food scraps that people like us left lying around. Suddenly I noticed that Lisa's face was a shade paler than before.

"What's the matter with you?" I asked.

"I just read a book all about bears," she snorted. "I was scared out of my wits about all the damage they can do. And their claws are extra sharp - I know because there was an ugly set of them on the cover of that book!"

Another thing that made Lisa petrified was the true story about bears in Maine that our teachers had taught us in school. Once upon a time, a man was out in the forest training his dog, which happened to be a boisterous beagle. Somehow, despite some fancy tracking equipment the man had, his dog just disappeared into thin air.

It turned out that the beagle was pulled down into a bear's den by the mother bear as she somehow thought that the dog was another one of her baby bears. The problem was that every time the beagle tried to make a run for it and escape the den to get back to its human master, the big nasty (or protective, depending on your point of view) mother bear just pulled it back in. Although that beagle finally did get away - with a little help from some helpful humans, Lisa thought that if this cruel fate could happen to a dog, it could surely happen to her too.

The day finally arrived for us to set out on our camping trip, our car stuffed with all kinds of equipment, including ropes, cords, pulleys, hooks, tarps, and other stuff that my dad had wasted a lot of money on and surely would never use. Unfortunately, we couldn't bring our dog as mom said he would most certainly tangle with whatever woodchuck, badger, or bear we'd come across. It's always hard to say goodbye to your dog, the protector of the universe - even if it's only for two weeks.

To be honest with you, we had a great time the first few nights. We got pretty good at setting up our tents quickly every dusk before we had a snack by the campfire. It was hilarious too when we woke up in the morning to see the perfect flat place my dad carefully chose for our parents' tent, compared to the slanting, root-infested slopes that Michael and I somehow managed to pitch our tent on.

But then Lisa had another shock when she noticed that the outhouse at one of the campgrounds had a simple design of a big bear paw on it. Michael and I thought that was hilarious: imagine sitting in a hot smelly outhouse and having a big bad bear come and knock on the door. On the other hand, this horrible idea just left Lisa's face another shade of pale.

It didn't help much that our dad insisted on wrapping up every long day that we spent driving, and then hiking on some gnarly rocky trail while being almost eaten alive by mosquitoes, with a session of scary stories by the sizzling campfire. But anybody who's ever been camping knows how cool and dreadful it is to tell and listen to scary stories around the fire, with a thin slice of the moon overhead, and all kinds of weird noises you've never heard before in your life coming from the shadows.

My dad had his own special way of leaving Lisa (and most of us) even more nervous by alluding to an ancient Bulgarian story of a mountainous village terrorized by a man-eating (or woman-eating, as the case may be) grizzly bear, with teeth as big as hunting knives.

The story continues with a group of hunters sent after the bear, together with a 12-year-old boy (my age exactly - but I wasn't scared, because I was sleeping in the same tent as Michael who I was sure would complain so much to any bear that came to our tent that it would just go away disgusted). The innocent boy's name was Yuri.

Anyway, according to my dad, the most dramatic storyteller ever: the Bulgarian hunters were all too fat to crawl into the narrow opening of the bear's den, so they sent the boy into the den tied to a rope with a gun in his hand. After a good while, when the hunters didn't hear any shots, they then pulled on the rope until a boy's body came out - with no head.

According to this crazy story, at that moment, suddenly none of the hunters could remember if the boy had ever had a head or not. The only thing they could think of doing was to go back to the village to ask the boy's mother. Yet she also wasn't sure if her son had had a head or not. But then, she remembered that he did have a head because she'd bought him a hat the year before!

Michael couldn't stop laughing when he heard the end of that story. But I could see Lisa looking aghast across the campfire, with her mouth just hanging open. I knew that our dad had really gone too far this time.

The next evening, Lisa said she wasn't feeling well, especially after a park ranger came to our campsite and told us calmly that a small but aggressive black bear had been recently sighted in the campground. To make matters worse, the bear had clamped his iron jaws on a sorry woman's backpack and run off with it.

The ranger warned us that we should never take any kind of food whatsoever inside of our tents, and on top of that, to leave anything that smells remotely like food (such as deodorant, lip balm, toothpaste, and candy) safely locked inside our car. In faraway Alaska, they have a particular way that you can haul your food up in a safety box between two trees so the bears can't get at it. But that system didn't exist here on Michigan's Upper Peninsula, the ranger kindly informed us.

Our dad thanked the informative ranger, and I looked sideways at Lisa - she looked like she was going to throw up at any second. Mom asked Lisa if she wanted to sleep between her and our father in their tent that night, but she refused (even though I'm sure she was scared - mom can't stand us saying this word, so I should say - stiff). That night, we didn't hear Lisa and Sally disagreeing loudly as they usually did before going to sleep. Instead, everything was eerily quiet.

You might have guessed what happened. The next morning, Lisa looked like death warmed over, an expression I read once in a scary book. On the other hand, Sally looked fine - in fact, she was snickering. Lisa started to explain that long after everyone else had gone to sleep the night before, she could hear the bear's claws clicking unmistakably on the pavement, getting closer and closer to her tent.

Terrified, she could hear the bear's breath exhaling forcefully as it drew ever closer to its target - her and Sally's tent, and its juicy contents - my two sisters! Finally, Lisa realized that the telltale clicking sound wasn't razor-sharp bear claws after all. Rather, it was the clicking of her portable alarm clock that she'd decided to bring on the trip. Michael fell off the bench at the picnic table when he heard that, and somehow, we all lived to see the light of another day.

CHAPTER 5.

YOUR TENT COLLAPSES AFTER MIDNIGHT IN A SWAMP

There's nothing scary at all about summer camp. Unless perhaps you and your pals' tent just happens to collapse or fall down, well after midnight in the middle of a swamp that's filled with vicious, blood-sucking mosquitoes, the odd snake or two, and lots of other pairs of shiny eyes that you still haven't learned how to identify.

That's one of the main reasons that you should pay close attention at summer camp when the trusty counselors give you a quick lesson on how to securely set up your tent. And that happens to be a keyword: "securely." Because anybody can set up a tent fast, especially when you have somebody helping you who knows what they're doing.

But if you're on a camping trip, and fooling around while putting up your tent, it may not go up so securely. My grandfather always said to me, "Haste makes waste!" Besides the fact that I didn't understand all the vocabulary - and sometimes my grandpa also spoke like he had a potato in his mouth - I understood at least that if you go too fast, you sometimes make mistakes.

Not to say that all mistakes are fatal, or that they may make you die. But you can suffer from a lot of unnecessary discomfort if you make those basic mistakes. Believe me - I've been there, I've done that, and I've made those same mistakes, and I did almost die.

So, if the wind blows hard at night while you're camping, or if one of your buddies' feet or legs happens to kick one of the tent poles out of position late at night, you may be in for a rude awakening. In other words, if you have to get up very late to try and set up your tent again with just a flashlight or two, good luck and God bless you!

What happened when I was ten years old, and I didn't really want to go to summer camp? I begged my parents to let me stay home and play with my little brother that June. It had been a long year, and I needed a break. I didn't really do too well in school, mainly because there was one kid in my classroom named Danny who was constantly bugging me. Whatever the teacher asked us to do, Danny was constantly interrupting, and he never let me concentrate.

I was so tired every day when I got home from school after a day of Danny harassing me. Other normal kids went out to play, while I just laid down on the sofa trying to recover. My parents didn't seem to want to help me - they just told me to talk to my teachers, and they'd work things out. My teachers told me to talk to my parents because from what they could see, Danny was doing his best, and he needed friends because he lived on a farm, far from school, and there were no other kids for miles around - just cows.

Another reason that I was tired at ten was that my coaches, my neighbors, my parents, and my teachers constantly told me, "Pay attention!" I was looking at them and listening to them, and they were still there, staring me in the face, and repeating like a drone, "Pay attention!" That's one of the reasons that I didn't pay attention when the camp counselors told me to pay CAREFUL attention when they showed us how to set up our tents. So, parents, pay attention: sometimes when you keep telling us constantly to pay attention, we do the opposite. OK, I'm glad I finally got that off my chest.

My parents told me that summer camp would help me grow and that I'd learn a lot and at the same time become more mature, whatever that was supposed to mean. My uncle was also crazy about the idea of me going to summer camp.

"That's the opportunity I never got when I was a kid," he said excitedly.

As a result, my uncle was always bringing me some useful gadget or another to take to camp, like a special waterproof flashlight that had different colors and blinkers, together with an atlas that showed all the states and was actually much larger than my backpack.

The only state we were going to was Massachusetts, not far from Boston where we lived. So, if my uncle had given me a smaller map, just of Mass - that might've been a bit more useful. My mom told me not to worry about her brother (my uncle) because he was much younger than all his brothers and sisters, and he was also a little weird, but goodhearted.

As much as I tried to get out of going to summer camp, my mom kept sewing my nametags on all my socks and t-shirts and underwear until I finally realized that there was no way I would be able to stay at home with my little brother, just being lazy and goofing off the whole summer. One thing I knew I would encounter at camp and that made me very afraid were moths - those creepy night butterflies that always fly and flutter into your face at night.

Sometimes when we came home late after going to the movies on a moonless Friday night, the moths would be swarming around our front door because my dad left the outdoor light. There were huge hairy moths, and little quick green ones too, and they all seemed to ignore the rest of my family and just focus on flying right into my screwed-up face. I used to start to hyperventilate when they flew at me, brushing against my nose, making me sneeze, trying to wedge their way into my ears, and some even flying down my shirt.

Another thing that made me scared was mosquitoes. I wasn't frightened of them because of the way they looked - they were nowhere near as scary and ugly as moths. But I had read an article for biology class that explained all the horrible diseases that mosquitoes carried like chicumbumba (or was it chikungunya?), dengue, malaria, West Nile, zika, and some others that I couldn't come close to pronouncing but that definitely killed a lot of people around the world every year.

How was it possible that an insect so slight and small could wipe out almost a million people around the globe in a single year? In fact, the article said that all the other murderous, scary animals combined - crocodiles, dogs, hippos, lions, sharks, snakes, and wolves - kill less than 100,000 folks in a year. To tell you the truth, I was pretty disappointed to find out that sharks only eat about ten sorry people per year.

When I finally got to camp, some of the activities that they had us do as campers were downright scary. Though to be fair to the counselors, they always gave us a choice: you could do the activity or not (except if you decided to skip that day's activity, they frowned at you a lot, and didn't talk to you quite as much during dinner).

The first, slightly menacing activity they invited us to do was called rock climbing. Now, if you were going to tell me that we'd scamper around on the top of some smooth rocks, or even jump around amid some big boulders, I'd be all over it. But this particular type of climbing was with a rope around your waist, and a flimsy helmet to protect your brain just in case you fell upside down, and the rope didn't hold you, from the top of the 60-foot cliff they proposed to climb up and down to us kids.

Well, I don't want to brag, but I've always been a good climber. Some people even called me a monkey when I was younger because I could climb into parts of some tall trees that other kids couldn't reach. Or maybe it was because of all the wild animal noises I used to make, which some people claimed sounded like a pack of out-of-control monkeys.

Anyway, this kind of climbing on steep vertical rocks was not something I could really brag about because my normal monkey moves didn't get me very far. Especially when I was reaching the very top of the 60-foot cliff, and the final move made me reach up and backwards to try to get over a kind of rock lip to safety, I started to breathe hard. It felt exactly like when I arrived home at night in summer and saw a million moths waiting for me in the lamplight outside our front door.

Sure enough, as I made my last-gasp effort to get over the overhanging lip, my hand simply slipped. The next thing I knew I was falling straight down, as fast as ever, until the rope tied around my waist suddenly caught and held. The system they called belaying, when they tied the rope around your waist and helped you with the cord secured somewhere above, actually worked. The big problem was when I say it worked, the rope squeezed hard into your waist, and then you were just hanging like a doll in the air - not close to the top or the bottom, but right in the middle of the cursed cliff.

Then, you had to swing yourself back over to the cliff, find a way to hang on for a precious moment and loosen the rope that was squeezing the life out of your middle. When you had your wits about you again, you had to climb the same cliff all over again, get to the top where you had already been, and attempt to get over that rock overhang once more. But this time you were really scared because you'd already experienced the firsthand terror of falling. However, since you were probably more scared of falling again, you usually made it over the lip somehow - which is what I did.

So, as you can see, it didn't matter if somebody talked to me that night at dinner to tell me I'd done a good job rock-climbing or not, because my stomach where the rope had squeezed it and my pride hurt too much to listen. And just like that, they told us the next day's special activity would be spelunking, which was basically the same as rock-climbing, except under the surface of the earth.

Let me ask you, and please be honest: of all the scary books you've ever read, and of all the horror movies you've ever watched, how many of them have taken place inside a slimy cave? A lot, right? Now you can guess how excited I was to go into a dark cave, probably the home to a million bats, moths, snakes, and spiders - but I guessed not that many killer mosquitoes.

The next day dawned bright, but soon enough we were far from the sun as our special camp activity took us straight to the gaping mouth of a huge cave, most likely with as many mummies as you'd find in an average day visiting the pyramids of Egypt. The funny thing was each camper was given the same flimsy plastic helmet to protect our precious brains that we used the day before for rock-climbing.

On top of each helmet, we had to fix a small headlamp that would illuminate our way underground - and I hoped wouldn't light up an entire moth's nest if there was such a thing. I knew there were wasp nests because my dad had tried to take one down from the side of the garage once using a ladder. He suffered a few stings but didn't complain too much (besides requesting three days off from his job). I wasn't really sure about moths. They seemed to be in all the dark, scary places that I could remember.

Our spelunking adventure began well enough as we could walk easily into the mouth of the cave. We soon got to a place not too far inside the cave where there was a bend in the passageway, and our lead counselor told us to be quiet and observe that we'd just lost contact with the light outside the cave. That's when some of the campers started to get scared, although I was still all right.

We were connected to each other by pieces of rope. Suddenly I thought: what if the counselors decide to commit a mutiny as I saw once in a movie, and just abandon all the campers deep inside the cave? Then, I figured that they probably wanted to keep their jobs, at least until the end of the summer, so they most likely wouldn't do that. After that, we saw some interesting stalactites and stalagmites - I can't remember the difference now, but they were both pretty cool.

After about ten minutes of walking inside the cave with our lights flickering (I sure hoped mine used Duracell batteries), we came to a thin horizontal gap which one of the counselors said was the entry point to a much larger cavern. It didn't look like any entry I'd ever seen in my life, mainly because you had to lay down on your stomach on the wet rock to crawl like a worm through that tight space. For once, I felt really glad that I didn't eat every single dessert I'd ever wanted, since I could see that some of the heftier kids were going to struggle wedging their way through that gap. But everybody showed how supple they were by squeezing in.

When we all finally got deep inside that thin crack in the rock way under the ground, one counselor spoke loudly: "Hey everybody, let's try to all turn off our headlights for one minute to see how we feel!"

I don't know about the rest of the kids, but I felt quite good with my light ON - thank you very much. Yet I went along with the program to show that I was a good sport.

Another thing I forgot to tell you about before was, besides my supernatural fear of moths, I had some other phobias that I didn't like to talk about too much. One strong one was called claustrophobia - the fear of small, tight spaces - and I was starting to feel a jolt of panic passing through my gut as we squeezed and wedged ourselves horizontally through that tiny, stuffy space. Wouldn't you know it - in my panic, I somehow knocked my helmet on the rock right above my head, and I heard my lamp just fizz out forever, with a snap.

I could still feel the person in front of me moving on the rope, but I don't have any idea what that person's name was. Petrified, I just held onto that rope for dear life, even though I knew nobody could pull me through that crack in the cave but myself. I've never been anywhere in my existence that was so dark - I couldn't even see the fingers on my hand one inch in front of my eyes. At that precise moment, I heard a person breathing hot next to my ear, with his or her light bouncing and ricocheting off the wet rock. Was that a murderer to put me out of my misery? No, it was just a counselor, asking me if I was all right.

A half hour and a lot of squirming later, we somehow made it back to the surface of our dear earth, and we could see the light flooding through the forest again at the entrance to that claustrophobic cave. I promised myself then and there that I would never have anything to do with a hobby or a job that forced me to go into a small, cramped space again, for the rest of my short or long life. At dinner that night, I got lots of slaps on the back from counselors and fellow campers. Did somebody think I actually did a good job getting in and out of that creepy cave or were they just acting like I was some kind of hero so that I could get through the worse camp adventures yet to come?

The next day, they announced that we'd need to walk on a wooded trail to a scenic place called Rutland Brook. There, we'd have plenty of time to set up our tents together with our camp buddies, and then have a fun evening around the campfire, with perhaps one or two ghost stories (or moth stories, depending on what scared you more), before a restful night's sleep. If that sounds almost too perfect - you're right - it is!

As I may have mentioned to you before, I was so worried about every kind of flying insect on the trail, and I smeared so much insect repellent on every small piece of my skin that could possibly be attacked by marauding insects, that I don't remember much of what we saw in that fancy forest. Someone later told me that we passed by a series of spectacular waterfalls, but I don't recall a single trickle as I was focused on beating back the entire insect world.

"Pay attention!" The lead counselor shouted as he and his assistant demonstrated how to set up their two-person tent capably and quickly. We were on a flat piece of ground that was near what they called Rutland Brook, which looked more like an overgrown swamp straight out of a dinosaur movie to me.

The problem again was that although I was paying full attention, our tent was a four-person one, which meant two things. One: we had four people alternately working together, and against each other, to set it up as quickly as possible. Two: ours was much bigger than the counselors' tent, and thus, if not set up carefully and correctly, was much easier to collapse in the middle of the night.

While I was swatting away at as many killer mosquitoes as I could, I found that one of my tent buddies was none other than Danny from school. Of all the terrible things that could have possibly happened to me at camp, learning that my arch tormentor Danny was sleeping in the same tent with me took the cake. He joked and played around as much as possible during the time it took to halfway set up our tent. Of course, by then, we were all busy waving and punching at the squadrons of mosquitoes that buzzed down on us in attack mode.

To make a long story short, we never finished setting up our tent properly because of all the joking and swatting going on. The announcement finally came for us to have a simple dinner by the campfire, and then a round of scary stories. Usually, the combination of a flickering fire and a spooky story or two will keep me up half the night. But that evening, I was so wiped out from walking all afternoon while battling enemy armies of mosquitoes that even the scariest stories seemed boring.

When we returned to our tent, I could see by the dim light of my flashlight that something looked very wrong. Our tent looked lopsided like it would fall down at any moment. Yet we were all - including the normally wild Danny - too tired to care, and before long, the other three beside me were snoring away contentedly.

Finally, I slipped into a kind of half-sleep, but I kept thinking and dreaming of mosquitoes carrying guns, knives, and bazookas. At some point, way past midnight, I'm sure, I woke in a sweat, with my foot burning like it was on fire. I shined my flashlight on the offending foot, only to see four fat sassy mosquitoes having a party on my ankle. With one massive swat, I swept them away, revealing four big welts where they bit, and a trickle of bright red blood dripping and running on the tent floor.

Tossing and turning, feverish from the bites, I kicked the corner tent pole hard by mistake. It was probably harder than the one goal I scored in soccer from outside the big box that year in school. The tent came crashing down on top of us, and rabid mosquitoes poured in on our bare heads. Groggy, rubbing our heads and arms, and saying every terrible thing you could imagine, my tentmates and I tried in vain to set up our tent again.

After 20 minutes of fighting with the poles and tarps and mosquitoes, we managed to return some kind of structure to the tent - but we were the receivers of hundreds of horrendous insect bites as a result. Believe me when I say that we didn't sleep more than a couple of hours, and I wasn't the most popular kid in the camp the next day. Strangely, Danny was quiet that day. In fact, he looked pretty sick and even left the camp early with one of his parents.

You'll never guess where I saw Danny next. Both of us were admitted to the hospital emergency ward a week later, both of us deathly ill with cases of something similar to malaria. But it wasn't malaria because that was a tropical disease that didn't exist in the cold state of Massachusetts! Even so, we moaned with high fevers, every kind of muscle ache you can imagine, and shaking chills that took over our weak bodies. We had symptoms that I wouldn't ever wish on my worst enemy. As I passed in and out of this feverish delirium, I could only remember that long ago, in a place far away, Danny didn't treat me too well. All of a sudden, that didn't seem to matter much, with the both of us almost dying together in the Intensive Care Unit at age 11.

"It's always darkest before the dawn," my uncle who gave me that fancy flashlight, for the camp he never had the chance to attend, used to say. I know the meaning of that phrase very well as one night I sank so low, and felt so bad, that I just didn't want to live anymore. But somehow, the next day, I got just a little bit better, and then, after a week of complaining in the hospital, I was even better and could laugh a little again. I also saw Danny, who was sharing the same room, smile a bit at me in return.

In the end, we both survived, and got stronger day by day. Danny went back to his farm, and I went back to my house, and we started our normal lives once more.

My dad told me one night, "I'm really proud of you—the way you matured at camp. You and that other kid Danny - both of you grew a lot through this experience."

After that, my dad slapped me on the back, and I could only think of mosquitoes. But, to tell you the truth, I'd already forgotten about moths.

CHAPTER 6.

I WANT MY BRAIN BACK!

Did you ever wonder, when you take a long-distance train, bus, or airplane, what people *really* have inside their private bags and cases? You probably think they're carrying clothes and simple things they bought, and in most cases, you're probably right. Do they have guns and weapons hidden away in their private belongings? Most likely not, because the x-ray equipment at airports would reveal them, and they wouldn't even be able to board the plane.

But did you ever imagine that the sweet old lady sitting across from you on the train, busily reading her book and sometimes looking curiously out the window, could really have a person's brain in that simple carrying case between her feet?! This is the scary story of one such lady who carried dead people's brains to hospitals and clinics without anybody ever suspecting her. It's also a tale about how kids suffer traumatic brain injuries, and how frightening this can be for everyone involved—especially the kids themselves.

If you ever set foot in London, one of the world's greatest capital cities, you may not be greeted by the best weather ever. It's often dark and gloomy, and the damp weather in winter can chill you to the bone. But you'll also find yourself in the best place for the perfect murder mystery, as well as the setting for one of the most haunting stories in the history of literature, *Dr. Jekyll and Mr. Hyde*, about a man who loses control of his alter ego, and finally his very life.

You're too young, but if you'd taken a typical train from the peaceful village of Cambridge to London back in the mid-1970s, you might have seen a small, well-dressed woman carrying a case a bit bigger than a hat box and waiting patiently at the station. In that carrying case was a human brain. Sometimes the brain was packed in dry ice to better preserve it, and when the brain left the skull of the person that died, it always expanded to fill a large carrying case. You see, when brains aren't inside our craniums, they get bigger.

In fact, this particular woman was only doing what was asked of her as a volunteer brain delivery person. A specialized doctor in Cambridge had asked her to hand-carry these brains from his clinic to another in London where they could be analyzed and studied. Many of the brains came from people who were only in their 30s and 40s when they died. That's a bit young to leave us here in this world and go to another, don't you think? The sad part was that these were unlucky victims of a brain disease called Huntington's Chorea.

The doctor told the woman, "When you take the train, please don't put the case with the brain in it up in the overhead bin."

You can imagine why he gave her this warning.

At the same time that the well-dressed woman was delivering brains in carrying cases on trains, there were also many bomb attacks happening in the UK, especially in the city of London, as terrorist groups tried to make their terrible political points in the worst, and least effective, way possible.

One day, while the small, older woman carried yet another brain in a case to London, she suddenly had to go to the toilet in the middle of the trip.

She asked a man in the next seat, "Would you mind keeping an eye on my case while I go to the restroom?"

The man answered abruptly, "Not at all, if you can kindly assure me that your case doesn't contain a bomb."

The woman decided NOT to say, "It's a brain, not a bomb." In fact, she said nothing at all, she just nodded and went quickly to the toilet. This story might sound to you a little like ancient history. It's all meant to introduce a more modern story that is just as scary, about a ten-year-old skateboarder who had a nasty fall, lost her brain for a while, but in the end, got it mostly back. Luckily, in the skateboarder's case, her brain never ended up in a carrying case on a train between anyone's feet.

You may know that skateboarding takes a lot of hard, repetitive practice, and a good amount of nerve. Even though Jen was just ten years old, she could never get enough of skateboarding. Especially after she'd seen her hero Rayssa Leal from Brazil win a silver medal in street skateboarding at the Tokyo Olympics at age 12, she simply had to go skateboarding every day, rain or shine, if she could. Well, when the sun was shining it was a lot better, but because that wasn't all too often in the fall, winter, and spring in London, she made the most of all kinds of weather.

Her father, an avid football fanatic, used to take her skateboarding at Crystal Palace Park. This was a perfect place for both of them - as a beginner, Jen could learn all kinds of moves and tricks from slightly older skaters, while her dad could slip into a nearby pub and watch his favorite club, Crystal Palace, play (and Jen noted, usually lose the match) on TV. After a while, Jen got better, and she started skating more at the more challenging Mile End Skatepark in London's East End.

This park had lots of crazy bowls, chutes, pipes and half-pipes, and smooth metal rails to challenge even the best skaters - kids, teens, and adults alike. It was funny to see adults try some more difficult skateboarding maneuvers because they almost always fell off their boards. And when adults fell, they went down in an awkward heap - arms and legs going in every direction, and their helmets usually flying off. What good was a helmet if it didn't stay on and actually protect your brain, the most sensitive and vital part of your whole body?

When kids fell, though, they went down fast, but normally bounced right back up as quickly as could be. It was almost like kids were trying to pretend that they didn't ever fall, or at least, they were hoping that nobody saw them, as their friends (and rivals) could poke fun at them and their falls later. Jen was getting better at skateboarding all the time, and she was also learning to fall. Her knee and elbow pads, along with her wrist braces, helped her sometimes. But mostly, her ability to slide and roll back up onto her feet quickly saved her time and again.

Obviously, the hardest skateboarding move was commanding your board so that it obeyed you to jump high up onto a descending metal rail, which you then slid quickly down. Actually, you plummeted down, much like a ripe apple falling from a tree - that was probably a better way to put it. Then, at the bottom of the rail, you had to move your feet and your board quickly so that you could land smoothly while staying upright on your flying board.

Also, when you tried such a dangerous move, you first had to strap your helmet on tighter, and try to block out all the distractions (which was hard as there were a lot of people talking loudly and shouting next to the biggest rail, especially when one skateboarder pulled off a monster move). In addition, you had to prepare yourself mentally, because there was a good chance you'd fall on the rigid cement. Falling wasn't a lot of fun. In fact, most of the time, it hurt.

One rainy day, Jen went to Mile End Skatepark with the vision of completing the most difficult rail jump ever firmly in her head. She'd decided that today would be the day and not even the light rain would stop her. There were fewer skateboarders that day because of the drizzle, and the sky looked especially ominous, with huge black clouds blowing in from the east.

However, Jen's heart was light as she repeated to herself, "I will complete this jump today. I *will* complete this jump today!"

She was agile and thin, just like her Brazilian hero Rayssa, and she felt particularly buoyant that afternoon like she was meant to do exceptional things. Jen's first approach to the rail was good, but she slipped in the rain at the last second. Her skateboard shot out from under her, and she fell hard on her back. A little confidence left her at that moment. Her second approach was better, but when she got to the middle of the rail, her skateboard went one way, and her feet another. She fell off the side of the rail and landed hard on her elbow and shoulder. Ouch!

At that point, doubt crept and crawled creepily into her mind. Can I really do this? Should I really be skateboarding, and trying this difficult rail move, in the rain? Should I have ever gotten out of bed at all this morning? Oh, it's terrible when your mind starts talking to you so much, bringing more doubt to the equation, and chasing away the supreme confidence that was there only a short time before. But her friends cheered her on as she approached the rail for a third try.

"Three strikes and I'm out!" Jen shouted back at them.

Her last approach to the high, slippery rail was a complete disaster. A raindrop landed squarely in one of Jen's eyes as she prepared for takeoff. She jumped high anyway, but the skateboard had a brain of its own. On that day, the board did what it wanted, paying little mind to its master. Jen could feel herself falling, almost in slow motion from a very great height.

Her instincts told her to brace for her fall with her arms and hands, but she fell strangely sideways and back and out of control. Her butt hit the wet pavement first, and then her arms tangled beneath her. Finally, her head snapped back, audibly cracking against the cement. Then, a wave of pain washed across her brain, and she remembered nothing more.

Jen's mom and dad had protected her as well as they could up to that point in her life. But, at a certain moment in our lives, we all must go our own way and make our own decisions. Some kids make better decisions than others. And some kids take up riskier hobbies than others: horseback riding, skateboarding, and trampoline jumping are right up there with the riskiest.

And why is it that some kids are luckier than others doing risky stuff, and seem to never get hurt? Jen had just cracked her head on the cement, after falling from a great height, while wearing a flimsy plastic helmet that didn't do anything to protect her super-sensitive cerebrum. Her brain had slammed into the skull that covers it and had definitely done some damage.

When Jen woke up, she was in a strange place, and some weird people were looking at her that she didn't recognize one bit.

"Jen, are you alright? We've been so worried about you!" One middle-aged woman exclaimed.

At first, Jen thought about what to say, and then how to say it. But the words didn't come out of her mouth as easily as they normally did. Finally, she stammered, "Who are you?"

"Oh, my dear darling girl - I'm your mother!" The woman blurted, almost crying.

At first, the skateboarding girl didn't recognize her own mother. Her head injury was so serious, so traumatic, that she'd lost some of her ability to speak her own language, and her memory had some big holes in it now. The doctors told her parents that this was called "traumatic brain injury" (TBI), and they should expect a long road back.

Jen had to stop school for a time because she couldn't keep up with her classes. She simply couldn't remember what she'd learned before. Initially, it wasn't so bad to get out of school for a bit, as some of her classes hadn't been all that interesting before - and she thought that now she'd also have more time for skateboarding. But not a single minute of skateboarding was allowed until she was completely recovered, said the docs.

Her main doctor had explained that it was normal for kids not to remember anything immediately after a TBI incident. The damage to her brain would continue to affect her short-term memory. The worst thing was that she couldn't remember very basic things in the beginning, like her friends' names, and what she'd learned recently in school, and she was also afraid that she wouldn't ever be able to jump on her skateboard again.

Even though her board had bit her like a wild dog or a venomous snake, she could forgive it - as long as she could somehow get back to the skatepark again soon, and practice again. On the other hand, the doctor warned her that it could be a good, long time before she'd be able to jump on her board once more. For the moment, she was like a fish out of water.

Her mother stayed by her bedside as much as possible, bringing her strength through her presence. A parade of friends came to visit her when allowed. But, after a month, her memory had only partially recovered, and Jen broke down and cried. In fact, she bawled her eyes out, and moaned to her mom, "I want my brain back!" Only her father could sometimes make her laugh a bit, talking about how bad his Crystal Palace football team was at the time, and how one player had stepped on the ball and fallen on his butt, in front of 50,000 howling fans.

Finally, late one night, Jen woke up with a start, scared and sweating. She'd dreamed that she faced three older, well-dressed women on a train platform. Each of them had a case between their feet, and each smiled slightly at her.

The one in the middle said, "Now, you must choose - which brain do you want to go through the rest of your life with?

Two of these three brains are defective. Two of them learn slowly and forget easily. Only one of them is truly a good brain. Only one of the three will allow you to learn and remember - and enjoy life with clear thinking!"

Jen started to cry softly to herself. Outside her window, the wind blew hard, and she heard hard drops of rain banging against the wall of her house. How could she get her good brain back? How could such a young girl, not even 12 years old yet, have to make such a weighty decision? Weren't these terrible decisions supposed to be made by adults and parents? Weren't girls like her only supposed to decide on what flavor ice cream to have when they went out with friends, or what color socks would match her skateboarding outfit?

In the end, Jen chose the brain in the middle.

It was between the feet of the nicest looking of all the elderly women. In fact, the way the well-dressed woman looked at her, so warmly and with a decided twinkle in her eye, made her look just like the Queen of England - a woman you could trust, a person who was always completely honest and open with you, a person who would have let you play freely with her corgi dogs until you had to go home to study at the end of the day.

When Jen woke the next morning, she remembered immediately all the things she had to do that day.

She suddenly remembered some formulas from her algebra class three months before that she thought she'd never fully understood. She still didn't remember all the vocabulary words on that list from her advanced English class, but at least she recalled most of them. Best of all, her mom and dad were smiling at her from their normal places at the breakfast table, the cat was drinking milk in its customary spot, and the sun shone down on all of London.

Little by little, Jen's memory came back to her, and she felt as if she was riding her skateboard down a slightly sloping ramp while exiting a dark tunnel into the brilliant sunlight. She never did try that rail move again, but that didn't matter because she started as a skateboarding volunteer, helping kids who didn't always have money to buy skateboards and all the pricey equipment required.

Best of all, she could clearly remember things again, and then one dazzling day, her dad's Crystal Palace side beat their archrivals, Brighton & Hove Albion.

CHAPTER 7.

ENJOY YOUR FIRST EARTHQUAKE

When I was much smaller, my dad got a great job working in Japan. I knew that this particular country boasts some of the scariest stories on earth, all about human-eating goblins, and muscular samurai warriors fighting against horrible enemy ghosts. Yet our real fright as a family turned out to be much worse when we tried to settle into "the Land of the Rising Sun."

Where we originally came from - the northeastern part of the USA - we had some pretty bad thunderstorms in the summer. But nobody had ever learned about, let alone experienced, a killer earthquake.

I don't mean to disrespect people who've already died or make you scared either, but soon after we moved back to the States again in 2011 when I was 12 years old, there was an awful magnitude 9.0 earthquake in Japan that reportedly took the lives of 16,000 people, and damaged or destroyed more than 400,000 buildings.

Well, you might ask me after all the years I lived in Japan with my family, what's your advice - how do you properly prepare yourself for a big, earth-shaking quake, especially when you start to lose your balance and fall, and have the pit of your stomach gripped by the most hopeless feeling you've ever had? To try to teach us something, my dad used to tell us a story about when he initially moved to Japan ahead of us.

He said he was staying in an old, small apartment, made completely out of traditional Japanese materials, like tatami straw mats for floors, sliding paper doors, and of course, lots of wood.

His host told him, "John-san ('san' was the honorific ending that polite Japanese people used to refer to adult men), if you ever wake up late at night, and feel your apartment shaking, then it's probably an earthquake." These were the words of his gracious host, Mr. Tanaka.

"Are you sure it couldn't just be a bad dream?" My dad joked in his typical way that was never quite that funny.

His host continued: "Remember that the first thing you need to do is immediately open the door because the door frame is the strongest part of your apartment. That way, if the rest of the apartment collapses, you still may be able to get out."

At this point in the story, Dad made an exaggerated funny face, trying to make us think that earthquakes were just a big joke, like Lego or child's play.

"Then," his Japanese host continued, "you should immediately turn off the gas line that you use for cooking. That way, if there's a fire - which there often is in an earthquake, by the way - your apartment won't blow up like a bomb."

By then, my father told us quietly, he was truly getting nervous.

"Finally," the host concluded, "jump under the table or the futon (the thin, flexible mattress the Japanese typically use to sleep on the sweet-smelling tatami floor) and maybe the roof falling down won't hurt your head too much!"

At that point in his story, Dad always abruptly threw all the pillows on the sofa into the air for special effect.

Then, just to wrap things up, our father told us three kids and Mom that the very first week he stayed in Japan while setting things up for our later arrival, there was a huge earthquake that hit the country in the middle of the night.

The lights were swinging overhead, the sliding doors were banging together, and the whole building was swaying back and forth mercilessly. So, our hero – Dad - quickly jumped up, still in his pajamas, opened the front door as fast as he could, turned off the gas, and finally hid under his futon until things got quiet again.

After a few minutes, he looked at the clock. It was 3:30 a.m.! He checked outside but heard nobody. It was absolutely quiet - like everyone was already dead from the quake, or at least they were still sleeping soundly. Yet, there was no fire, no smoke, or any fire engines.

So, in the end, he crawled back into bed and slept a few fitful hours. When he woke up, he was dying of curiosity.

"Tanaka-san, what happened as a result of that colossal earthquake last night?" Our dad called his host to inquire.

"Oh, don't worry, John-san. That was a very small earthquake - you'll be fine," his host reassured him.

Following that quake, Dad told us, one day he went to look at a new apartment with an agent. While he was inside the living room of the new apartment, he could feel that unmistakable shaking sensation again.

He shouted in a panic to the agent, "It's a big earthquake! What should we do? I don't see any futons to hide under!"

The agent calmly replied, "Please relax, Mr. John-san - it's only the *shinkansen* (bullet train) passing by on the tracks nearby!"

After our family had lived in Japan for a while, we all had to admit that there were many different things compared to our homeland. Of course, the money and the language were hard to understand, especially when you had to try to memorize a lot of stick figures to learn to read.

They called the stick figures letters, but to me, they all ended up looking almost the same as each other! Then there was the public bath on our local street where people went every evening to clean themselves so much that they almost scrubbed their skin off. But be careful - you could only use your soap in the shower at home, never in the communal bath!

Some restaurants had plastic models of every kind of food inside. So even if you couldn't remember the Japanese words, you could still point to the pictures on the menu or take the serving person to the display case and physically show them what you wanted. My favorite kind of restaurant had a conveyor belt that constantly carried fresh sushi and sashimi on small plates, right past your nose as you ate. It reminded me of my toy train set when I was a kid!

Dad was always going out to eat at expensive restaurants with his Japanese clients. One time, he said a client insisted that he eat a dish called "dancing shrimp." The shrimp were literally still alive on his plate - they were still moving! But then, when you put a little bit of soy sauce on them, they died, and you could eat them. We all thought that was disgusting and scary.

Another time, our father said he told a special client he was a little tired of eating so much raw fish every week. So, the client took him to a unique restaurant that served raw fish, as well as raw chicken and raw horse! My mom's face got all twisted up when she heard that story because she loved horses more than any other animal on earth. My dad said something silly about how we have to learn to be more flexible in life.

When I was 11, and a student in a multinational school in Tokyo, our teacher assigned us a book of Japanese ghost stories that were translated by an American living in Japan at the turn of the 20th century. His name was Lafcadio Hearn, and the book was called *Kwaidan: Stories and Studies* of *Strange Things*. Just the name of the book made me shudder. I used to take it to bed late at night and read under my covers by flashlight, which made the already scary stories even more terrifying.

One day, we were invited to an event in a big skyscraper in downtown Tokyo. It was so cool to go in the high-speed elevator all the way up to the 50th floor, although my mom didn't look so good. I mean my mom always looked good, but she was afraid of heights, so her face turned a sort of strange green color when we went whizzing up so high in that elevator.

The parents went off in one direction to listen to some speakers and eat finger foods (and I hope no fingers!). The kids went in another direction where they had a lot of games spread out on the floor and tables, as well as some stations where you could trade Pokémon cards while talking to other Pokémon lovers (like me!).

I'm not sure if I said to you before that when an earthquake suddenly starts, there's no warning at all. At least, when we suffered from those alarming thunderstorms back home, they started small. They soon got really big and nasty, with howling winds - but you still had some time to adapt. In an earthquake, all of a sudden, the world around you started moving and shaking, and things started falling and fissuring. There was definitely no way to get ready for the shocks to come.

I remember to this day, I was talking normally to a boy just like me who was crazy for the latest generation of Pokémon, in particular one character called Squirtle. Before we knew it, the tall skyscraper we were in started to sway to the unmistakable rhythm of a giant earthquake.

But rather than stop quickly, the movements just kept getting bigger and bigger, and it seemed like the large building was getting ready to take off like a rocket. All the books and magazines and games on racks came crashing to the floor, while people all around began to scream and wail. I cringed when I saw folks losing their balance and falling out of control all around me.

I don't really know what happened next, although I do remember that I was too frightened to run. Besides, there was nowhere to run to! Then something hit me hard on the back of the head - harder than any time I was ever hit by any so-called friend on the playground, and even harder than one time when I was ten and got hit by a baseball right on top of the helmet that I was luckily wearing to bat.

After I got whacked, the next thing I saw was blurry images of big dark crabs crawling and scuttling toward me. They had horrible-looking human faces on their backs, just like in the horror story by Hearn that I'd been reading the night before.

It seemed like the wind was blowing hard inside the skyscraper, and then I could hear the sharp sounds of an ancient battle. Not only were there women and children screaming at the tops of their lungs, but also terrible cries from a war between violent armies pierced the air.

Just as quickly as it began, the earthquake slowed and then ultimately stopped. I found myself laying in the arms of what I guessed was a nurse, speaking to me in a language I couldn't possibly understand. Still dizzy, I felt the back of my head, and there was a big wet bump.

From close by my side, I could hear another man speaking English firmly to a person trapped by a mass of debris.

The man was saying, "Don't give up hope - just stay calm where you are. The fire brigade will be here soon to help you and all of us out of this mess."

Then, miraculously, I saw the faces of my mom and dad anxiously peering down at me. Even though I'm not a very emotional kid, I couldn't help but cry my eyes out, mainly in relief that we were all still alive and together.

We'd survived an earthquake that we later learned was more than 7.0 on the Richter scale. The bump on the back of my head disappeared after a few days. But believe me: the memory of that massive earthquake that made everyone fall down and that shook all the skyscrapers in Tokyo will probably never go away.

Lucky for us, the buildings there are built with the best technology on the planet. They're created to withstand quakes since they're designed to sway and flex like the fastest-growing and most flexible plant in the world, bamboo. Maybe my dad wasn't completely wrong when he said we all need to learn to be more flexible.

CHAPTER 8.

DANGEROUS DOGS SNAP AT YOUR HEELS

More than any other pet, I always loved dogs when I was a kid. Most of them were cute and playful, and my best friend's dog was an example of a completely obedient one. That canine possessed the ability to do all kinds of tricks (although my other good friend's dog was a funny breed called a Beagle, and it used to howl all the time - like it wanted to turn into a coyote or a wolf under the full moon at any moment).

And my favorite aunt had a Corgi which was so smart that it learned how to play soccer by stopping the ball with its nose, as well as herding everything in sight - other animals, children, bees that buzzed past in summer, and even the airplanes that flew over a few times a day.

But not all dogs are man's best friends, as they say. I'm here today to warn you about the scariest dogs that exist, like Dobermans and Rottweilers. Those breeds would be just as happy tearing the skin from your limbs as chasing a ball or a bone. In fact, you should know that once upon a time, Rottweilers were used to pull the meat in carts to markets in Germany. That means the Rottweiler breed of dog used to do the same work as a bull!

When I was a kid, there was a cute show on TV about a type of dog called a Rough Collie. The specific dog in that program was called Lassie, and all it did was save the life of a sailor, then the lives of two boys lost in a snowstorm, and finally, it played with orphaned children on a farm. This kind of Collie never seemed the least bit scary until I was riding my bike past the neighbor's house after school, and he suddenly released his Lassie-like Collie, which quickly came in hot pursuit of me.

Luckily, I was only about three blocks from home and rode my bike faster than any kid in recorded history. But that Collie kept coming after me, all the way to my house, barking and nipping at my heels all the while. In the last stretch of road just before the relative safety of my driveway, the Collie made one desperate lunge for my foot on the bike pedal, with its medium-sized, very sharp teeth. Somehow it didn't sink those teeth into my delicious Achilles heel, but it did get a good mouthful of my white sock.

Safe in the bathtub later, with one holy sock as proof of my frightening adventure, I started to imagine that dogs were inherently good, but they could be trained to be bad, like the German Shepherd dogs we always saw in old movies which served as vicious, ever-snarling guard dogs. Later, I saw real films about how the police trained and turned these rather large, unpleasant creatures loose to punish criminal people on the street in certain situations.

After talking to some other friends about my theory, another 12-year-old told me that his Uncle Al had been innocently walking once on a remote dirt road in the countryside at the base of the mountains. Suddenly he noticed a large, dark animal bounding across the meadow, and coming directly at him, at an alarming speed. As the mysterious animal drew rapidly closer, my friend's uncle could clearly see that it was none other than a Doberman Pinscher dog, with no human master of any sort in sight.

The Doberman Pinscher surely has the reputation of an extra aggressive dog, with very large teeth and jaws slightly smaller than a shark. Uncle Al didn't like the idea of getting eaten alone by a large dangerous dog in the countryside. However, even though he was a fast runner - in fact, he was a former college track champion - he reasoned that he wouldn't get far with this four-legged biting machine close behind him.

Somehow, Al had bought a new harmonica recently that fit snugly in his hip pocket. Although he only knew how to play one simple song on the harmonica (also called a mouth harp), he stood still in the meadow with his eyes closed and started to blow hard, repeating the only song he knew as the crazed animal came ever closer.

When he finally mustered the courage to open his eyes, he met the steely eyes of the Doberman, which was five meters in front of him. Uncle Al never stopped playing that one out-of-tune song, and never moved an inch from where he stood until the somewhat pacified Doberman ultimately went loping back in the same direction it came. All right, I realize that this short story doesn't really prove my theory - all dogs are basically good until they're trained to be bad by people. But now, you're probably a bit more scared of dangerous dogs in general, right?

Then, let me tell you about something even scarier called a stray dog. How do these animals become stray, which is when they live in packs in the forest or some out-of-the-way place in towns or cities? These dogs have to survive on the street or in the forest because people abandon dogs. They get rid of the dogs they don't want because they've grown too big, or they bark too much, or they bite a little when they get excited, or the people who first wanted a dog decided that they don't want that cute animal anymore.

Dogs don't usually run away from home. Normally, dogs love their masters, even if the canines are sometimes treated badly. Sadly, many dogs are rejected by the very people who once wanted them as cute pets. Do you think that gives stray dogs any reason to ultimately want revenge?

Peter was a kid who really loved dogs. He lived at the end of a dead-end street. Behind his house, there was a dirt road that went some distance into the forest. Peter's dad told him never to walk, run, or ride his bike down that dirt road - but not because wild animals or ghosts were waiting there to snatch him away. Rather, Peter's dad told him that there was a pack of scary stray dogs living somewhere near where that road disappeared into the dark forest. They weren't exactly wild, but they seemed like it. They sometimes chased joggers and snarled at people out for a simple Sunday walk.

However, like most kids that age, Peter was overcome by curiosity. He wanted to know what stray dogs looked like, and how they acted and sounded because he adored all kinds of dogs and was always pestering his parents to get him a pet dog.

His dad only said, "Dogs are fun, but they're expensive. And when you get a little older, you're going to lose interest in your pet. Then your mom and I are going to need to take the dog for a walk, take the dog to see the vet, make sure the dog's constantly got water and food in his bowl, and you know, we're just too busy for all that."

One day after school, Peter rode his bike to the end of that dirt road but didn't see a single animal. He rode slowly, listening to the breeze in the treetops, and various songbirds making their merry sounds. On his way back though, he started to hear some growls, and then a group of snarling animals got closer and louder on both sides of the road. There was no doubt that they were angry dogs, but he never saw a single hair or snout or even a tail wagging behind a bush. Just as he was leaving the dirt road, Peter felt a big dog brush against his leg but saw nothing.

After riding all the way home in a panic, Peter called his best pal, Kirk, and persuaded him to ride together the next day to try and discover the phantom dog pack. They rode quietly to the end of the road, and sure enough, they heard the unmistakable snarling of a pack of dogs, yet still saw nothing.

This time, as they reached the end of the road, and the invisible snarling reached a deafening roar around them, Peter felt something tugging on his sock. He still saw nothing, but he and Kirk heard the horrible growling as an invisible dog took a bite out of Peter's white sock. They rode their bikes like mad to escape. Peter had a hole in the heel of one sock, and the spit of a dog dripped from it, but they decided not to tell their parents - even though Kirk at first insisted that they should.

But the two were braver than even they thought. They called a third friend, Deb, to join them the next day on the same scary phantom dog bike ride. This time, they rode slowly until they heard the snarling of stray dogs coming from the forest. There was a bend in the dirt road where the snarling was the loudest, and even the road dust kicked up showing the presence of something. Still, they saw no dog, but the barking and growling and snarling got closer and sounded worse than ever.

Peter was the bravest and liked dogs the most of the three. He stopped his bike, and slowly got off. He held his hand down and out to an imaginary dog. At that moment, the three kids heard a loud yelp. Something had bitten Peter on the hand - blood trickled across his palm.

"Don't worry - I'm fine!" shouted Peter with a tear in his eye.

The phantom dogs had suddenly gone quiet, and the dust on the road had settled.

They all checked Peter's hand and saw four distinct tooth punctures, one of which had bright red blood seeping out. Deb's idea was to wrap a bandana she was wearing around the wound. When they got back to their neighborhood, the three were sufficiently scared and decided to have a secret, emergency meeting. Soon after, they all approached their respective parents.

Although they never told their moms and dads what happened that afternoon to Peter, and how he'd been bitten on the hand by an invisible dog (that would've sounded a bit strange anyway), they all pestered their parents more than ever. Finally, all the parents agreed to go on Saturday afternoon to a place nearby called the dog pound. There they could examine and pet and talk to stray dogs that had been recovered in their town.

Soon enough, Peter, Kirk, and Deb were all the proud owners of stray dogs. Now and then, they'd go together to a local park (they called it "The Dog Park") to chat and play, and they would all swear that their three strays had been good friends in another place and time. By the way, whenever they rode their bikes down the dirt road where their parents warned them never to go, they could now only hear the breeze in the tall pine trees.

CHAPTER 9.
THE ZOMBIE HITCHHIKER

As a kid, the easiest way to get from one place (Point A) to another spot (Point B) is to ride a bike, walk, get a ride, or perhaps hitchhike. That last one means you stand by the side of the road, stick out your thumb in the direction you want to go, and hopefully, soon enough, some nice person will stop and pick you up. They'll kindly ask you where you want to go and try to help you get as close as possible. At least, that's the theory.

But no parent in their right mind would ever permit you to hitchhike. It's much too dangerous, they'll say. You could get hit by a car standing on the side of the road. Or worse, the driver or other passengers could do terrible things to you, or you might get kidnapped by a child-napper, and nobody would ever see you again.

And what about the drivers who pick up hitchhikers? What exactly are they looking for - new friends on the road, or maybe some company to help pass the time on a long trip? Maybe they're really trying to help somebody standing by the side of the road with their thumb out who's cold, lonely, or penniless, to arrive in a better place. Whatever their intention is, they're definitely not looking forward to picking up a zombie hitchhiker.

To begin with, not everybody's completely clear on what a zombie is or isn't. Some people say that a zombie is a person who's already dead but lives again at night - you may also have heard the super-scary name "the living dead." Other people say that a zombie is a person who has no soul or spirit of their own but is controlled by magic or some other powerful outside force. A few people say that a zombie is somebody who's extremely tired, like your dad when he gets home on Friday night - `that's not so scary, is it?

Many parents tell their kids never to hitchhike. They usually don't mention zombies, but rather they emphasize the danger by telling their children one of the scariest true stories ever about the risks of picking up hitchhikers. One such story is about a woman named Maggie who picked up a hitchhiker while driving on a lonely stretch of country road.

When she stopped, the rider immediately threw his bag in the backseat and got in. Maggie greeted him warmly, asked him his destination and some polite questions, and treated him like a long-lost friend. The rider seemed shy, but he smiled and nodded a lot in response to Maggie's questions. When the hitchhiker got to his destination, he thanked Maggie profusely for her kindness. He asked if it were possible for Maggie to give him her phone number so that when he was settled in his new residence, he could repay her for her kindness.

Maggie agreed, and after a week, she got a call from the hitchhiker. However, he sounded completely different. He wasn't nice at all, and told Maggie in a loud, threatening voice that when he first got in the car, he had imagined doing many terrible things to her, but only stopped short of those horrible deeds because of how nice she was to him! Remember: your parents are right to tell you never to hitchhike or pick up a hitchhiker.

One more scary story, especially if you're lucky enough to hear it on Halloween night, or late around a dying campfire, is about the innocent man who picks up a young hitchhiker who turns out to be a ghost. The man saw a thin figure hitchhiking at a dark corner near the local cemetery on his way home late one night. He stopped to give the person a ride, and the figure got in quietly beside him. It was raining hard, and despite his attempts at conversation, the hitchhiker only said, "10 Capen Street, please," in a soft, sad voice.

When the man stopped at a traffic light, he could see the soft features of a 12-year-old girl, he guessed, staring straight ahead. She might have been crying, the man thought, or her face was wet from the rain. After he dropped her off at 10 Capen Street at a house surrounded by spooky-looking pine trees that swayed in the wind, he went home, only to find that his rider had left her hooded sweatshirt in the car.

The next night after work, the man swung by the unlit house at 10 Capen Street. He waited a good long while at the front door after ringing the doorbell. Finally, a frowning older woman answered, and the man offered the sweatshirt that the girl had mistakenly left in his car.

The woman looked suddenly shocked, and said, "This belongs to my granddaughter who was hit by a car a year ago while walking near the cemetery!"

After that disturbing tale, you may not be in the mood to hear too much about zombies. But just for fun, and to make sure you're sufficiently scared of hitchhiking for the rest of your life, here we go. A mother was driving her ten-year-old son home from school as the sun went down, and they saw what appeared to be a mother sheltering her child from the swirling snow while hitchhiking on a winding, mountain road.

The ten-year-old exclaimed, "Mom, I think these people need our help. It's so cold outside, and they look like they're probably freezing!"

The mother replied, "If your father were still alive, he'd never agree to this, but I think you're right. I'm going to stop and give them a lift."

The woman stopped the car some meters further down the road where there was a little space to pull off the road in front of a huge snowbank.

As the hitchhiker and her child struggled to open the car door and get inside, a blast of arctic air and snow crystals blew into the opening. When they finally managed to close the door and sit upright in the back seat, the boy and his mother noticed a red glow in their eyes.

The hitchhiking adult hissed, "We're survivors of the apocalypse, and we desperately need food, or we'll soon die!"

The boy happened to love all kinds of science fiction and had recently fallen in love with a game called "Wasteland" in which he'd scavenged for supplies while fighting off a variety of mutant animals.

"Mom, can we take them to our house for pizza? The least we can do is try to help them out of their jam!" The boy begged his mother.

"But we don't want pizza," croaked the child hitchhiker menacingly. "We need human flesh to survive."

The mother knew that they were slightly in trouble at that point. But as most mothers are, she was a quick thinker (and also a fan of online apocalypse games), and said, "Don't worry - there's a mall just ahead where there are a lot more people - even on this dreadful snowy night - and plenty of delicious human flesh for all of us."

The pair kept quiet in the back seat, though their eyes glowed more fiercely than ever.

As they drove on the snowy road, they saw more and more cars stopped, stuck, and crashed in the snowdrifts, while groups of other zombies increasingly appeared. The mother was an expert driver, however, and she slalomed the car past the other wrecks and slid into the mall parking lot just as the zombies in the back seat began to moan and pant with the expectation of a human flesh feast.

The mother pulled recklessly into a parking spot just in front of Walmart, grabbed her son by the arm, and raced inside the store, straight to the section where they sold Halloween costumes. The zombies moved too slowly to pursue them.

The boy finally blurted out, as he gasped for breath: "Mom, what are we doing? How can we possibly escape this zombie apocalypse?"

"If you can't beat them, then join them, son!" The mother exclaimed as she found some tattered but fashionable jeans on the sale rack.

They then sprinted to the makeup section with her son just a step behind. She smeared bright red lipstick all over her face and then her son's so they both looked like they were zombies themselves covered in blood.

"Your father never did like Halloween too much, but for all his faults, he was right about one thing - never, ever pick up hitchhikers," the mother lectured sternly.

CHAPTER 10.
SWIM OR SINK

I always thought I was a pretty good swimmer, even though the first time I ever took a swimming lesson as a five-year-old with my older sister at the YWCA, I just sank immediately to the bottom of the pool. At the same time, my sister simply floated, nodding and smiling at everyone.

The lifeguards decided to rescue me from the pool bottom with a big metal hook. That wasn't really necessary, and I got totally scared seeing that evil hook coming down right at my head. But then again: you can't cry under the water, can you?

When I was ten years old, I thought I was an even better swimmer than ever. My parents went as far as entering me in a race, and I swam very quickly - my arms and legs churning in the water like fast-motion propellers. The only problem was that when I arrived at the end of the pool after my assigned length, I was far behind all the other swimmers, leaving my relay team at a decided disadvantage.

Then, when my parents decided to send me away to summer camp with the sister I mentioned earlier, on the first afternoon we were instructed to jump immediately into the pool in the pouring rain for a waterlogged swim test. What's worse - they said the idea of the test was to prove that you could survive if your boat had an accident in deep water!

So, you had to take off your wet, super-heavy jeans while you were trying to keep your head above water, tie the legs of the jeans together while attempting to swim, and finally fling them in the air above the water to catch some air in the tied pants legs.

Then, the jeans could possibly serve as a kind of half-inflated life raft. Not only did that sound totally ridiculous to me, but in reality, it was almost impossible to do. Of course, my sister did it successfully in about a minute, and was already out of the pool and completely dried off by the time I finished - gasping for breath - soaked to the bone from the cold pool and the freezing rain.

Later, I asked a camp counselor: "Why did we really need to do that kind of crazy swim test? Why couldn't we just put on life jackets like everybody else on a normal boat?"

He replied curtly, "Sometimes the camp counselors and directors are a little smarter than the campers."

Anyway, if you've never seen anybody drowning, or fighting to save their very lives in the water, I'm sure you can find a video about it on YouTube. Actually, don't bother. It's not very pretty. In fact, it's downright awful. I almost drowned twice when I was a kid. One time at the beach, it was the end of our summer vacation, and the waves were getting bigger and bigger as more storms piled in from the agitated Atlantic Ocean.

My dad, who was a lifeguard as a teen, (although my mom said he never got paid though sure got a lot of attention from girls near his lifeguard stand), told me to always swim directly in front of our designated umbrella. That was kind of hard, especially when the waves got progressively nastier and carried your little body quickly down the beach.

But the best feeling in the world was body surfing with success, and after a long ride, getting churned around in the surf, and then somehow finding your feet on the sand just before the next huge wave crashed on your innocent head.

Yet the scariest occurrence in the wild sea was something called a rip tide. That was a place along the beach where the water went fast out to the open ocean, and took everything floating along with it - garbage, leaves, and sticks we called driftwood, as well as the bodies of little boys and girls. Once, I got caught right in the middle of that terrible rip tide. I recall clearly that I was swimming as hard as I could to get back to the beach, but my body just kept going farther and farther out to sea on the swirling tide.

When I finally tried to shout for help, I mistakenly swallowed a bunch of salt water. I knew I could only hang on for a minute longer before I descended forever to "Davy Jones's Locker," which was a terrible place on the ocean floor that I'd read about in a chilling book full of horrific pirates and all the murders they committed for gold and greed. That book was named *Treasure Island*. Of course, it's not really a locker, but rather the final resting place for drowned sailors and travelers!

Miraculously, I didn't drown on that occasion. Luckily, another lifeguard had been paying attention and saw me in distress. He swam hard to save me at the last second as my head was going under the choppy water for the final time. Ultimately, the kind lifeguard led me right to our family's beach umbrella. I was crying, shaken, and thankful - all at the same time. And my dad was mad at me. I'm not sure if it was because he wasn't the one who saved me, or if it was because I didn't follow his orders. Or maybe he was upset that I didn't actually drown! Sorry - my dad's better than that - I admit.

My sister also told me that her best friend had related the tale of her Uncle Mitch. He also almost drowned when he fell out of a canoe on a lake at night after he and his friends drank a lot of wine. If you know anything about canoes, they never sink. They just keep floating - unlike the big ships you see in movies like *Titanic* and *The Adventures of Pi* that go straight to the bottom of the ocean in massive storms, together with all the innocent people and sad animals onboard.

Uncle Mitch fell out of that canoe with his big hiking boots on. Of course, those boots immediately started to pull him down under the water. Apparently, he was a good swimmer too, but wine and water don't mix well, and he wasn't wearing a life jacket, and then, just like me, he took a big gulp of water by mistake.

In fact, according to the story, he was trying to laugh when he took that shocking gulp because the canoe just spinning around endlessly in the water as he tried to get back in was such a comical thing. Amazingly, Uncle Mitch was also saved at the last second, by a close friend who happened to come along in just the nick of time in a rowboat.

Did I tell you that I almost drowned twice? The last time was the worst, and I'm not really sure why I'm still here to tell you this story now. However, when I was 12, I made some friends at the beach. They were an inseparable couple: a brother named Linus and his twin sister named Lily. With names like that, you'd think they would be sweet and innocent. Actually, they were. But their older brother Walt turned out to be the devious one.

One fine summer day, they invited me to eat lunch at their house on a canal not far from the beach. I went off on my bike without asking my parents - my first mistake. When I arrived at their cottage, I noted that nobody except the kids was home. Linus said simply that his parents always went out in the middle of the day and left the kids home alone. Whatever - we had a simple lunch, and then Walt asked us all if we wanted to go for a ride on the family's shiny motorboat.

My second mistake - I said yes, even though Walt was going to operate the speedboat, and he was only 14 years old. In addition, there wasn't a parent or guardian in sight. To tell you the truth, I don't really know what a guardian is, although they use that word a lot when talking about movie ratings, and there may even be a pro baseball team now called the Guardians (though I think they're just guarding first base and not all the wayward kids like me in this world).

Walt revved up the boat engine until there was a lot of black smoke and riotous noise filling the air at the dock. Soon enough, we had a nice speedy ride through some crab-infested canals until we got to the middle of a beautiful wide bay filled with sparkling water - who knows how deep it was.

Then Walt cut off the engine, and shouted, "Who wants to go for a nice quick dip?"

I'm not sure if you already know, but my first name is Dave (like in "Davy Jones's Locker").

"Hey, Dave, why don't you jump in and test the water for us?" Walt barked at me.

I didn't hesitate - in I went, without thinking, finding the water cozy and warm. While my head was under water ever so briefly, I heard the engine suddenly start up, and when I surfaced, I could see the boat shooting off toward the horizon.

At first, I thought, *what kind of joke is this?* Then I thought, *I'm sure they'll come back soon. After all, they're my friends!* (Even though I'd met them for the very first time just that summer.) Next, I tried to float on my back like I'd seen my sister do ever so easily hundreds of times.

The only problem was that she floated effortlessly while my legs kept dragging me down under the water. They wouldn't stay flat on the surface - as hard as I tried. Unfortunately, I was dressed only in a pair of shorts and wasn't wearing jeans so I couldn't try to use that useful survival skill I'd once learned all about at summer camp.

I concentrated on dog paddling, but I could feel I was getting more and more tired - even though everyone told me I was very athletic - at least on dry land. I don't really know to this day how many minutes passed, but I do know that my mind started to play tricks on me. I could see lots of my favorite sea animals, like seals and turtles, and even some brightly-colored snakes, coming to check on me, and saying things to me in that weird way you hear sounds underwater. They seemed to be smiling, but they disappeared soon after into the watery depths.

People always say: "If you are ever dumped in the ocean, don't panic!" I remember that I didn't panic, but I also knew that the end was getting near. I thought about my dear family, and all my good friends back home, and realized I would never see them again. I think I even started to cry, but I was underwater, so I don't rightfully know.

Then, suddenly, I could hear the strangely distorted whine of an engine approaching under the sea. I struggled to the surface, and I could make out a shadowy form motioning to me from the side of a boat. I'll never know how I managed to climb onboard, having almost just drowned, but then I heard a high laughing voice.

"How was the water?" Cackled Walt.

Some things you never tell your parents, or anybody else, for that matter. You don't tell anybody because those are your very own personal scary secrets. I can only tell you one thing, which is an old expression you probably already know: "Look before you leap!" After all, you're still too young to go to Davy Jones's Locker.

CHAPTER 11.

YOU LOST YOUR BROTHER?

My parents once lost me, completely. My mom tells me I always liked to wander off as a tot. Then finally, one day in winter, I disappeared into "Rabbit Country," which was a wild, bushy area not far from the beach. The main problem was that they lost me without a trace, and I was only two years old. I disappeared into thin air, and my mom said she (and maybe my dad too) almost had a heart attack.

My dad used to mess up a lot, mainly because he was always thinking about a thousand different things at the same time. He was supposed to be watching me, while my mom looked after my four-year-old sister. The excuse that my father used, when they discovered that they'd lost me, was: "that little guy moves so fast - I can never keep my eye on him!"

There was no choice but to leave my mom and sister there, as my dad rushed off to get the police in person (back in the days long before we had cell phones). My mom said it took them almost forever to return on that cold, windy afternoon, and she had plenty of time to imagine all the horrible things that could have happened to me: eaten by wild animals, caught in the quicksand that sucked people down to a slow, ghastly end, or carried away by huge prehistoric birds to their faraway nest. Well, at least you need to give my mom credit for having such a good imagination!

Eventually, my dad returned with a veteran policeman, who was also an expert in tracking animals. He could follow the signs in nature that showed where animals had recently passed, like tufts of fur or hair or feathers they'd left behind, footprints or tracks in the sand and mud, as well as dried, or still wet, blood that showed where a predator had feasted on its unlucky prey. The police guy quickly followed my tiny boot prints and after only five minutes of searching, found me - stuck in a large bush, unable to move back or forth due to my huge winter jacket.

In the end, this particular story had a happy ending. Apparently, I didn't even blink, nor did I say anything at all to my dad or mom. I just looked at the knee-high black boots of the policeman, and said, "I want a pair of boots just like those!" When the adventure ended with this remark, my dad laughed nervously, and my mom started to cry her eyes out, while my older sister just stood there, wondering what the fuss was all about.

Have you ever seen those sad, scary photos on the subway or the bus in your city showing people who have somehow "disappeared"? Their parents and families and the police are desperately looking for them, but after weeks and months and then years pass, and those dear friends and family members in the photos don't reappear, they are really given up as "lost." The scariest thing is that they usually show the lost people smiling in the photos like they just went to the corner store, and they'll be right back.

I already told you that my dad, despite being very smart, is a bit distracted - you might say that he's good at losing things, like his car keys and eyeglasses and favorite pen. Just to let you know that there was another time when he lost me - his only son - again, but this time in the vast blue ocean. He tells the story extremely well when you ask him to, but you can see in his face when he recalls what happened that he's partly embarrassed but mostly nervous about how he almost never saw his son again.

When I was three years old, my dad begins the story, we went to the beach where the waves weren't necessarily too big, yet they were breaking hard and fast. I was playing in the surf, wearing some simple arm buoys, more to identify me in the water than actually help me swim, or save me from drowning. As the waves grew increasingly bigger, reaching my chest, I continued falling headfirst into each wave I could - obviously having the best time of my life, according to my dad.

My father was right behind me, he claims, helping me get to my feet in the surf after I was tumbled around by each wave. But, at one precise moment, when my dad was perhaps distracted by a surfer falling in the distance, or maybe by thinking of one of his two hundred business projects which never made any money, he said that I simply disappeared under the water. When I fell into a larger-than-usual wave, and the surf became white with agitation, my dad felt for my body under the water directly in front of him, but there was nothing there - only water.

At that point in the story, my dad counts to ten out loud, which I guess is supposed to make the story more dramatic - because that was the amount of time I stayed under the water before suddenly popping up like a plastic toy in the calm bathtub. Usually, everybody laughs at this crazy story, mainly because I'm still here on the face of the earth to laugh at the story too. But you know that when you lose things that you like, it's terrible. However, when you lose a person in your family who you love a lot, it's much more than terrible.

So, this is the story of how I lost my little brother. I forgot to tell you that when I was four years old, my baby brother was born. His name's Bruce, and at the same time that he's just about the cutest kid in the world (at least according to everybody outside my family), I'd like to crack him in the head with his plastic milk bottle sometimes. Of course, I'm just kidding - I would never do that to my sweet little brother - especially if my mom happens to read this story in the future.

Why my parents put me in charge of my little brother when I was six and he was two, I'll never know. We went on a long car trip, and naturally, we had to stop the car every two hours at either a gas station, or one of those big car and truck centers on the highway, which has bathrooms, restaurants, stores, a place for your parents to get some coffee, and even a place to walk your dog or cat, as the case may be.

At the time, my sister Julie was old enough to take care of herself. Even so, she didn't want to have much to do with us younger boys because she was basically wrapped up in her own private world. She talked mostly to my mom, and not so much to the rest of us. As usual, my dad was responsible for us two boys, but he had to calculate and consider the gas and oil and correct change for the highway tools, and if his coffee had enough milk and sugar in it or not.

As you might imagine, when we stopped at this massive rest stop on the superhighway with thousands of cars whizzing by every second, my dad said to me, "Dan, you need to take care of your little brother Bruce for a minute because I've got a lot of things to think about."

I looked at my baby brother Bruce, whose face was red and smiling, and was probably the only person in the world who had more energy than me, and who had the desire to go somewhere every minute of every day unless he was sleeping.

So, there we were, in the middle of this big combination restaurant store where you don't know anybody except your family, and everybody seems to be extremely busy and rushing around to buy or eat something before jumping back in their cars and continuing their long road trips. There's nothing really scary about this kind of place full of loud, mostly happy people, except if you get lost yourself, or if you lose somebody much younger and more vulnerable than you, who you're supposed to be looking after, by the way.

One minute, I was watching my dad filling his favorite travel mug with steaming coffee, dumping about five cubes of sugar in it, and then swirling it all around with a bunch of milk, with my baby brother right by my side. The next minute, my brother Bruce was completely gone, and all I could see were hundreds of people going in all different directions at the same time, and the front doors of the place wide open, with the sun blasting in, and the high-speed freeway just a few hundred meters away.

I froze in fright, and my dad looked at me square in the eye: "Where's your baby brother whom I told you to look after?"

I could only cry and say, "Dad, he's gone! I don't know what happened - he was just here one second before!"

Rather than immediately get angry at me, I was surprised to see my dad leap into action, almost like a superhero, although he was still wearing his regular clothes. He left his coffee mug on the counter, grabbed my hand, and headed purposefully down one corridor and then the next, searching high and low for my little lost brother.

Bumping into every possible person in his way, my dad accelerated down the last corridor that had all the chocolate bars and cookies and candies, which seemed to me that could fill all the Halloween sacks in the world. Sure enough, there was Bruce, sitting on the floor, surrounded by a growing mound of chocolate packages that he'd pulled down off all the shelves. He laughed when he saw us, and then my dad scooped him up in his big arms, and I thought he'd never put him down again.

Two years later, when I was eight, our teacher asked us to write about the time in our lives when we were the most scared. This was our English homework just before Halloween. Some kids wrote about haunted houses, while others wrote about imaginary monsters under their beds, or in their attics or basements. One kid even wrote about how scared he was when he went to the doctor and had to get a simple injection in his skinny arm. For me, the most scared I ever was? When I lost my little brother.

The teacher told me that my composition was fantastic because it seemed so real.

I said, "Well, it was!"

She gave me a short story to read about how a farmer and his wife had a baby boy that changed their lives and brought so much happiness into their home. Suddenly, one night, the baby's crib was empty - he had disappeared - or was he kidnapped? Everyone in the community went looking for the baby, and somehow, another farmer found him crying at the bottom of a dry drinking well. But he was fine - without a scratch.

The parents were so relieved, and they watched the baby carefully every night, for at least one month. Then, late one night, the farmer discovered that the baby was gone from his crib again. His wife cried uncontrollably until they found the baby, again unharmed, but bawling his eyes out at the bottom of the same dry drinking well. They then decided to bring in a special priest, who performed something called an exorcism to drive away some kind of evil spirit, and the baby grew up, and the family lived happily ever after.

That was a pretty scary story, I admit, but I thought mine was much better, especially because I'll never forget the look of utter relief in my dad's eyes when we found Bruce once more - after I'd lost my baby brother. I forgot to say that after we found Bruce, my dad lost his favorite travel coffee mug.

He just said, "It's not so easy to replace your favorite mug. But it's a bit harder to replace one, or two, of your sons. Now, where are my keys?"

CHAPTER 12.

LIGHTNING TRAVELS THREE MILES

Did anybody ever tell you that if you're in a storm that has lots of lightning and thunder after you see a lightning bolt flash in the sky, you can count until you hear the thunder to find out how far the dangerous lightning actually is from you? Of course, if the lightning bolt rips through the sky near your unprotected head, and then you hear a violent clap of thunder immediately afterwards, you know you're in big trouble.

You should also know that lightning can travel up to three miles. That means that lightning, which can kill you or me in an instant, can fly through the sky for up to five kilometers, depending on where you're reading this. If you're playing outside when lightning starts to flash across the darkening sky, or even worse, if you happen to be in a swimming pool when lightning shows its awesome force in the sky above, by all means, get out of the pool and find cover immediately. If you keep playing or swimming with lightning flashing in the air, you could quickly say hello to an early grave.

Just to make you sufficiently scared, about 20,000 people die every year from lightning strikes around the world, according to that famous magazine, *National Geographic*. In fact, the chances are NOT very high for you to get struck by lightning at all during your lifetime. But surely you know that if you're outside in a storm, then your chances are MUCH higher than if you're inside, safe and warm!

There was once a soccer game in Congo where 11 players were killed by lightning and dozens more watching the game were also struck. But, can you guess which outdoor activity every single year leads to more people being struck by lightning than any other? If you guessed fishing, you're pretty smart. That's why you can imagine how terrified I was when my uncle insisted that he and I continue hunting, even in the middle of a horrific summer thunderstorm that had some of the biggest lightning bolts ever in the history of mankind (at least that I saw in the 11 years of my life!).

In fact, we weren't hunting in the traditional sense of the word. We were really scouting for large deer on an island where my relatives have a cabin. First of all, you might like to know how deer get to an island. Do they take a boat? I asked the very same question to my uncle who grew up close to the coast, and who always visits islands for various reasons: boating, fishing, grilling and eating the fish, kayaking, scouting wild animals and birds, and best of all - according to him - sleeping better than any other place in the world, because there are no airplanes, cars, or trucks to bug you. Instead, there are only lobster boats passing by at 5 a.m., together with plenty of sweetly chirping birds, insects, and the odd coyote.

Anyway, my uncle told me that at one point, a single deer swam to the island.

Then, as a smart 11-year-old, I asked, "Doesn't it take two deer to have a family so that now there can be many deer on the island?"

My uncle was a funny guy, and he said something like, "I stand corrected. At one point, two deer swam to the island, and now there are many deer, even on this small island, because there's a lack of natural predators to trim the population."

I have to admit that my uncle was impressive with all his tricky vocabulary. He even told me that another time, a couple of lobstermen were on their boat in the early morning peering through the fog, when they saw a horse swimming in the ocean between two islands. When they got a little closer, they realized it was not a horse, but that very peculiar animal called a moose, due to its large, protuberant nose. Just going out for an early-morning swim in the freezing ocean between two islands!

My mom had already warned me that her brother - my uncle whose name was Oliver, but we called him Uncle Ollie - was head over heels for wild animals, and he had all kinds of fancy camera equipment to hunt and capture them. My uncle also told me that for one month every year (I think he said October), there was a real hunting season for deer on the island, and it was possible to see some strange chairs attached to trees about five meters up the trunks, where the hunters sat and waited to startle the deer as they wandered by.

I always felt that hunting was cruel to the animals as they were shot with bows and arrows, or guns, and they didn't really have a chance. Then, their beautiful lives of jumping and running and playing in the island forests came to a quick, tragic end. But my uncle told me that now - because the deep population was out of control since there was a lack of predators - hunting was necessary to cull the population. Every time, my uncle had a scientific explanation for everything. But that was fine, because I want to be a scientist, and help save the world with science. My uncle says I should actually be a "mad scientist," and maybe he's right!

What was really great and scary at the same time was that my uncle and I stayed alone in that small wooden cabin for almost a week, and there was no electricity or running water. If we wanted to take a shower, we had to fill these big plastic bags called sun showers that had one transparent side and the other was black to reflect the sun and heat the water (although it took about two hours to get hot). Then we hung the sun showers in a nearby tree and had a quick rinse, while the birds flew by, and the squirrels chattered in the branches.

At night, we had our dinner by candlelight because there were no electric lights. I don't know why, but the food tasted so good, even though we had some really simple dishes like spaghetti with ketchup (when my clever uncle forgot to buy tomato sauce at the store). My uncle said that our sense of taste was "heightened" (better) because of all the fresh salty air we breathed there, and all the exercise we got every day scouting for wild animals like deer, fox, and porcupines.

Of course, after we ate dinner, and played a few card games, my uncle's eyes got wider, and he started to tell me scarier and scarier stories about predators and their prey, and the web of life, where one animal (or sometimes he slipped in the example of a shark eating a seal, a marine animal we also saw frolicking in the bay) ate another. He told me legends from the islands involving ancient spirits, and people whose houses were haunted by ghosts - some even friendly - that lived there long before.

One night, just as he was getting to the climax (that's the interesting part) of another great ghost story, a sudden wind blew out all three candles on the table simultaneously. Uncle Ollie quickly turned on the headlamp he was wearing attached to a headband, and his face looked more evil and stranger than normal in that weird light that partly showed his face and glistening eyes. That particular night, it took me a lot longer to fall asleep.

The island life was sure exciting. Even taking the organic garbage we had generated, like apple and banana peels, and the many paper coffee filters filled with dark brown coffee grinds from the liquid my uncle drank all morning, to the compost pile - only ten meters from the old house down a short forest trail - was a kind of adventure. That's because my uncle told me to pay attention to the exact positions of the leftover food that we'd thrown there the day before. Usually, raccoons or other small animals would come to feast on the compost pile at night, especially when we were lucky enough to have juicy lobster for dinner, and we threw the lobster shells on the compost pile.

Though we never saw them face to face, the raccoons had a blast with the lobster shells, flinging them around and scattering them far and wide (away from the compost pile) so they could extract every last piece of sweet lobster meat. What made me slightly more frightened was when Uncle Ollie told me that it wasn't only the innocent masked raccoon that came to the pile late at night, but other bigger, more aggressive animals, like the bobcat and coyote that local people had heard howling to the full moon in the early morning hours.

The morning that I woke up after a nightmare about a bobcat and coyote fighting for a lobster shell against my uncle and me, Ollie reminded me it would be our second to last day on the island. He said he planned to take me to a big meadow where we could possibly see deer grazing and playing at dusk (just after the sun went down). Later, we set out for the meadow, hoping to see the wild deer - I'm sure I was much more anxious than Uncle Ollie.

The early-evening shadows played tricks on our eyes as we walked quietly through the forest. When we came to the wide meadow, we witnessed a perfectly quiet scene: tall grass lined by softly swaying trees, and in the distance, the shape of one deer energetically bounding into the forest. My uncle said the deer were "skittish," which he explained meant that they were easily spooked or scared - just like me on Halloween, or when I heard Ollie's dramatic tales by candlelight.

We walked all the way to the end of the big meadow, but only saw one other wild animal - a fat, happy porcupine asleep on a big branch of an apple tree. I would have never seen this dark brown circle of an animal, but Uncle Ollie knew where to look, as an experienced islander and wild animal tracker. Many apples were scattered below the tree, and we imagined that the porcupine had a bulging belly full of applesauce.

At one point, we heard some kind of animal crashing through the bushes and trees. Ollie told me it must be the same deer, running to escape us. We circled back on the trail, and when we'd almost arrived back at the house, I noticed another trail going in a slightly different direction.

"Uncle Ollie, can we walk down this trail just a little? Maybe we'll see something," I said excitedly.

It was much darker then, but he agreed. Only a moment later, I felt his hand grab my shoulder, and heard him issue a loud "Shhhhh!"

He pointed directly in front of us, and only five meters away stood a tall deer, perfectly motionless, with only its big ears twitching to catch any sound we made. It didn't move an inch. I realized I hadn't taken a breath for about 30 seconds in the excitement, but then decided to wave at the magnificent animal. It didn't have any horns or antlers but looked to me to be as big as a horse. It probably wasn't used to people waving at it from a distance of mere meters, so it turned and leapt and twisted in midair, disappearing immediately into the shadowy forest, with its white tail flashing goodbye.

That night, I slept like a rock, with no bobcats or coyotes visiting my dreams - only deer, all running and jumping preposterously high, in slow motion. The next day was sadly our last on the island. So many adventures, and only the biggest one is yet to go! Did I start telling you about lightning before, and how terrible it can be? Sorry that my story skips around so much. I guess I'm just a normal 11-year-old kid.

On our last island evening, the weather had changed dramatically, and dark clouds rolled in low over the ocean. We heard thunder in the distance, and just at the time we were planning to make one final visit to the meadow scouting for wild animals, terrible bolts of lightning ripped across the horizon. On this occasion, Uncle Ollie was more anxious than I about going walking in the storm. He told me everything would be fine, and that all we had to do was count - if the lightning came too close, then we'd quickly return to the safety of the house.

That turned out to be a very bad idea. When we got to the edge of the meadow, the wind was whipping, the thunder was rumbling all around, and flashes of lightning came from every direction we looked. I was super scared and hid under Uncle Ollie's big arm - maybe if lightning struck him first, I would somehow escape. We counted together, and it seemed like the lightning was getting farther away because when we saw the flash, we were able to count to almost ten - which meant that the real storm was almost ten kilometers or miles away - I already forgot which is bigger, a mile or a kilometer?

No matter - the next lightning bolt came out of nowhere. It sizzled dangerously, directly over our heads, and hit the same apple tree where the porcupine napped the day before. The tree exploded into a million sputtering sparks. I sure hoped that the slow-moving porcupine was far away by now!

Uncle Ollie shouted, "duck!"

I knew he wasn't yelling about a bird that quacked. Rather, at that exact moment, a huge branch from another tree hit by lightning almost fell on top of us. I thought briefly of the story where the chicken says, "the sky is falling!" and wished I was home, safe on the sofa. But then, the lightning got less and less, and the rain decreased a little.

One last flash of lightning illuminated the horizon, while directly in front of us one deer sprinted past, and then another, and then a third - all running as fast and jumping as high as anything I'd ever seen. Finally, a fourth deer, a bit behind the others, rocketed across the meadow, clearly not wanting to be left behind by his buddies.

When we eventually got back to the house, soaked to the bone because of the storm, Uncle Ollie made us some hot chocolate, which hit the spot. I shook from the thrill of the four-sprinting deer, and the fact that we were almost done in forever by lightning.

My favorite uncle then lit the three fat white candles sitting in the middle of the table, and calmly said to me, "I don't think you probably want to hear any scary stories tonight, do you? By the way...you can tell your mom about the deer, but don't say anything about that lightning in the apple tree five meters above our heads, OK?"

CHAPTER 13.

HALLOWEEN HAVOC

Not everybody likes Halloween, obviously for different reasons. Personally speaking, I love it, mainly because I've got a massive sweet tooth, but also because dressing up in a costume is fun, and the whole thing can be a little scary also - depending on how much havoc or craziness you run into on that peculiar night at the end of October.

Some parents don't really like Halloween, maybe because of their religion, the fact that they need to buy a lot of candy for the neighborhood kids, or the possibility that somebody will play a trick on them - though that usually doesn't happen. My parents say that I need to turn over the candy to them when I get home from trick or treating so that they can control the amount of sugar I eat.

My friend's dad deals with it simply: he just demands 20% of all the candy that his kids bring home. I'm still learning about percentages at school, but that seems like a pretty good deal for my friend.

There's one Halloween, in particular, I'll never forget. It happened when I was only eight years old. Now that I'm practically grown up at age 12, I don't think I'd feel so bad about the havoc that I experienced then. The first problem was that my Spiderman costume kept falling down over my eyes the entire night. That was terrible, first because my mom spent hours making that costume for me at home and second because Spidey needs to be able to see well to shoot webs at people and also to collect candy.

Even though my mom stayed up almost the whole night before Halloween, making the costume that I didn't really want to wear anyway (I wanted to be Dracula), she was mostly worried that as trick or treaters, we'd get run over by a bus or a car, or that maybe some crazy person would decide to kill all the kids in our neighborhood by handing out poisonous candy.

Neither of these things happened in the end, but it did start raining, and when we finally came home, all our candy was completely wet, which was actually good because then our parents weren't in such a hurry to take it away from us. But my favorite sweet called candy corn basically melted in my trick-or-treat bag.

That made me really disappointed because I always thought that candy corn had more substance. I mean, I really thought it was more real - not just a bunch of sugar and artificial coloring. I could still lick the melted candy on the bottom of the bag, but it wasn't so much fun.

That year when I was eight, Halloween was on a Saturday, so we got to stay out trick or treating until later. We also saw one car crash into a telephone pole, but luckily none of us - my dad said it probably crashed because more people get drunk on Saturday nights. We also saw one house on fire, maybe because a candle inside a pumpkin burned out of control and caused a small accident. Anyway, we were smart and didn't go trick or treating at the burning house.

The worst thing that happened early in the night was to one kid in our group who carried a glow stick he got from his parents so that the cars would be better able to see him at night. The problem was that the glow stick broke, and somehow the kid got the liquid in his eye. He was crying like crazy because his eye was burning. He also shouted out that he would probably lose his eye. But finally, at one house, they took care of him and washed his eye, so he didn't cry and shout so much anymore.

Naturally, before we went out trick or treating that year, our history teacher in school wanted to make sure we knew something about this ancient festival. He said it all started when some guys named Celts who were living in the UK about a thousand years ago (and were not directly related to my favorite NBA basketball team called the Boston Celtics) celebrated their new year at the end of October. It was the end of the harvest after all, and everything was cool, but at the same time, they believed there were also spirits wandering around in the middle of the living. Yikes!

One of the hardest and scariest things for kids to do – obviously - is ring the doorbell of somebody's house who they don't know at all, especially if the place has flashing lights, and is decorated with all kinds of scary things, like spider webs, rubber rats in the corners, unreal bats (although some of them are still moving), black cats with hunched backs, and witch paraphernalia (another new word I learned in school, and probably will soon forget). Unfortunately, I couldn't see all of this stuff because my Spiderman costume kept falling over my eyes as I told you before. But I did see one other kid practically jump out of his costume when he rang the doorbell to one house, and a two-meter-tall Frankenstein character answered suddenly.

According to our history teacher, the people in Old England even used to put bowls of food outside their doors to keep the ghosts happy. With all these crazy things going on, you would think that some kids would be so scared that they would never want to go trick or treating again. But our teacher told us there's some kind of chemical called adrenalin that our bodies produce when we get scared, and somehow it usually makes us feel stronger and less afraid.

Let me make a long story short and tell you about the Halloween havoc that I really experienced at the finish of that fateful night when I was eight. We went to one house at the end of a dark street, and since our bags were already basically bursting with candy, we decided that it'd be the last house on our trick-or-treat tour for that night.

I don't remember who rang the doorbell, but it wasn't me because that house gave me the creeps. I'm not sure why, but there was something not quite right - my Spiderman intuition told me to be careful. A person finally answered the door wearing a mask I'd never seen before in any store. Most of the kids stood back - nobody was really interested in rushing into that house to check the candy options.

A man's voice came from behind the mask saying: "We only have enough candy for five kids, and the rest of you need to go away."

I wasn't that scared and saw that I was the fifth kid from the door, which soon slammed shut behind me.

The man told us in a shaky voice, "we're going into the next room to get your candy. But don't be alarmed - there's something there that maybe some of you would prefer not to see. Let's check how brave you are."

Normally, I thought of myself as brave, but something about his voice made me shiver, and then my Spidey costume fell over my eyes once more. Sure enough, in the next room, which was considerably darker, there was a big table covered with candy. Yet, there was also a real coffin - although it was closed - I mean the real wooden box that they put in a hole in the ground in the cemetery when people die.

The man continued, "I'm sorry that this coffin is here now, but my favorite relative just died, at an early age."

At that moment, the four kids in front of me all grabbed a handful of candy from the table and ran for the door.

I stood there alone, right next to the coffin.

The man looked me directly in the eye from behind his horrible mask, and whispered, "You're welcome to see what's inside."

Instantly, I realized that I had enough candy already, and I didn't really want to know what was inside that all-too-real coffin. "No thanks! And keep your candy!" I blurted.

Lucky for me, my Spiderman costume didn't fall over my eyes at that precise moment. And I was happy that the adrenalin the teacher told us about allowed me to run all the way home, without getting hit by a bus or car. It took me about four years to recover from that very special Halloween night. But now that I'm 12 years old, I think I'm ready to try trick or treating again.

CONCLUSION

Thanks a lot, all you kids, for coming along on this frightening ride with us. We hope that you didn't decide to read these 13 scary stories long after dark, in the middle of the darkest part of winter, or just before the scariest festival on the calendar called Halloween.

If you were brave enough to finish all of them, congrats to you. And if you weren't really scared by the stories about clicking claws at Creepy Campground, lightning that travels three miles just to find you, or the worst thing that could ever happen to anyone at Halloween, then the chances are you won't be scared by much in this world at all!